# MANNERS AND MONSTERS

MANNERS AND MONSTERS BOOK 1

TILLY WALLACE

Print edition ISBN: 978-0-473-47910-7

Published by Ribbonwood Press

www.ribbonwoodpress.com




To be the first to hear about new releases, sign up at:

www.tillywallace.com/newsletter

**1**

---

*arch 1816. London, England.*

Life did not bestow her gifts with an even hand. There was so little in Hannah Miles's favour that, in the quietest moments, she wondered if she had been overlooked by the Fates entirely. She possessed neither beauty nor fortune to make her a desirable catch, and her most constant companion was solitude.

Once, her father had been the brave surgeon saving the lives of dashing military men on the battlefields of Europe. That brought a modest number of social invitations, as other women thought Hannah could pass on love letters to wounded officers. Then tragedy struck their family and Sir Hugh Miles turned his focus to the research of Unnatural creatures and their diseases, which earned him the moniker, whispered discreetly, of *mad scientist*.

Hannah's engagements became few and far between when it was known she assisted in her father's research and even handled his test subjects. She wasn't certain whether it was the stain of employment that made her unacceptable, or the risk of contamination escaping her father's laboratory. Perhaps they feared that Hannah harboured a contagion in the folds of her clothing or catching a ride on her bonnet. Regardless, social invitations were in scarce supply when your peers feared a plague-ridden rat would jump from your reticule and spoil the scones.

Her mother, Lady Seraphina Miles, had once been the most powerful mage in all of England, and as such, held a rank equivalent to that of a duke. However, magical ranks were only bestowed on the mage and did not pass to family or descendants. That meant her mother's position and any associated privileges had been lost upon her untimely death.

To add to society's misgivings, Lady Miles still resided in the family home.

There were simply too many blots on Hannah's name for society to know quite what to do with her. Far easier to omit her name from invitation lists entirely. Few missed her and she had no desirable skills to add to an evening. Life had not blessed her with a fetching singing voice or skill with a musical instrument.

This invitation was a rare exception.

She ran a finger over its rich, embossed paper. Her dearest friend, Lizzie—Lady Elizabeth Loburn, daughter of the Marquess of Loburn—had become engaged to a most handsome young duke. There would be a grand ball at the Loburn mansion to celebrate the engagement and soon there would be the society event of the year—the much anticipated wedding.

Hannah had no such expectations of marriage. There were no suitors knocking on the family's forest green door and no prospects on the horizon. Some women were born to be the darlings of society. By dint of their beauty, wit, or talents, they dazzled others and were the centre of attention. Lizzie was one such woman, exceptionally beautiful and with the voice of an angel.

Then there were women like Hannah, whose place was in the shadows, applauding a performance or holding a shawl for a much-loved friend. Not everyone could be a star. Some people had to be the night sky, the dark background that allowed the star to shine.

While some women became bitter at never finding a place in society, Hannah greeted her prospects with quiet acceptance. The world needed spinsters to be companions, nurses, or governesses. Like any young woman, her heart ached to know true love, but she knew she was loved by both her parents and her friend. That would suffice, even if their love didn't quite reach all the empty hollows in her heart.

"Have you said good night to your mother yet, my dear?" A booming voice echoed through the house.

A wistful smile touched Hannah's dusky pink lips. Papa didn't give a fig for society's conventions. She could picture him standing at the bottom of the stairs, his gold pocket watch in one hand as he tapped his toes with impatience. It didn't matter that they were supposed to be late; he would hustle her out the door and away so that they reached their destination *early*. Oh, the horror.

Her mind skittered away from that word and her smile dropped. One hand went to her breast, her fingertips resting lightly on the primrose yellow silk over her heart. So many unseen horrors existed in the world. How she wished to return to a time when her only experience of *horror* was being the first to arrive at a dance!

Thousands of years of magic and dark arts had fundamentally changed their world. A rift had opened with another mystical world, allowing creatures to seep through and walk the earth. Those who did not follow the rules of Nature were called Unnaturals—creatures outside the normal realms of humanity.

Others, like her mother, were called the Afflicted, and things that once had only resided in fairy tales and ancient myths now expected invitations to soirées or lurked in the dark to snatch the unguarded.

Smile in place, Hannah rose from the padded stool, picked up a gossamer-thin green shawl, and left her room. The soft satin slippers on her feet made no noise as she walked the short hallway and then took the wrought-iron spiral staircase upward. The balustrades were carved to resemble a vine and she felt like an adventurer climbing to a dangerous and unknown world above.

At the very top of the stairs was a small landing and a large panelled door. Hannah rapped on it.

A chill washed over her skin as she grasped the door handle and pushed into her mother's tower. The atmosphere was charged with electricity that made her hair prickle on the back of her neck. Whispers rose from the bed—words of power that circled the high ceiling like ravens caught in thunder-laden clouds.

Silence fell, and the storm vanished as Hannah crossed the rug.

"Hannah!" Lady Miles looked up, her features and expression obscured by the thin muslin veil covering her face. The fabric rested on her shoulders and brushed against her collar bones. Death had taken a cruel toll on her mother, but she was still a part of family life.

Hannah's gaze glided over the end of the bed and

the blankets that lay flat against the mattress. She tried to concentrate on her mother's face, or what she could see of it.

"Oh, my child, you look exquisite." One gloved hand went to her mother's chest. Then she patted the spot next to her.

Across her mother's lap rested a wooden tray, specially constructed to hold a book open at the right angle so the invalid did not tire herself holding it up. Lady Miles could bend the elements to her will, but magic took a physical toll on those who sought to control it.

Hannah sat on the blanket and drew her attention away from her mother's too-short frame by glancing at the old tome, a book on the history of the dark arts in Europe. While her father laboured below their house, using science to find a cure for her malady, her mother used academic knowledge. In her tower she pored over ancient books, seeking a magical way to undo the curse that had struck down more than two hundred noblewomen.

"What were you doing?" Hannah asked, curious about the tiny clouds that had scudded into the corners of the room.

Lady Miles closed the book and rested her hand on the worn cover. "Would you believe finding a way for farmers to bring rain to parched crops?"

"No, I would not. England is not known for its lack of rain."

A gentle laugh blew the veil outward. "Your father and I labour on the same problem, but we approach it from two very different directions."

"Which is no real answer at all, Mother. Why do you not let me help you more?"

Maternal bonds of protection chafed. Hannah longed to be a full partner in her parents' study, not merely an assistant. As the first descendant of a mage, Hannah was devoid of any magical ability, but she still had a keen mind.

"Because I do not wish to burden you any more than we already have." Lady Miles reached out and took Hannah's hand. Linen hid every inch of her mother's skin. The long gloves disappeared under the sleeves of her nightgown. Three years ago, her mother had been struck down by an assassin as the French tested a most terrible poison. Their weapon had only stilled her heart, not her mind.

"It is no burden to find a way to restore your health," Hannah said.

Nor was Lady Miles the only sufferer. What everyone referred to as the *Affliction* had invaded the finest parlours in London. An innocent-looking jar of face powder had been perverted by the French into a terrible weapon. Of the *ton*, or upper ten thousand, over two hundred women and a handful of men had been struck down after dusting their faces with cursed powder. Thankfully the sufferers were a small percentage of nobles and an insignificant number compared to London's population of nearly one and a half million souls.

"Enough of maudlin thoughts. You must promise me that you will have at least two dances tonight." Her mother's voice was softened by the fabric covering her face. "One dance with your father, because the old goat needs the exercise, and at least one with a young gentleman."

Hannah smiled at a request that seemed near impossible. Her father would disappear into the library to discuss business, and none of the gentlemen would notice her.

Her mother gently shook their joined hands. "I will not have you trying to disappear into the wall hangings, Hannah. A young woman should dance and laugh at a ball."

"I will try, Mother, but I make no promises." She kissed her mother's hidden cheek and then stood. "Likewise, I would ask that you do not overtax yourself."

A soft chuckle blew the veil a few inches. "When death finally claims me, I shall sleep for eternity. Until then, I continue my study. I have a letter for Kitty if you do not mind delivering it, along with the entertainment she requested. The letter is with the box over there. Do not open it until the exact moment arrives."

"Of course, Mother." Hannah slid the thick enve-lope into her reticule and then tucked the wooden box under her arm. It was about the size of a small hatbox and equally as light. She wondered what her mother had concocted for the evening, but her curiosity would have to wait.

Hannah closed the door as her mother's clouds gathered above her once more. Both her parents possessed a rather large stubborn streak, and neither would be dissuaded from their chosen path. Her mother would whisper arcane words until she collapsed over an open page.

With one hand on the railing, Hannah wound her way back down to her impatient escort.

A broad smile wrinkled her father's face. "Ah, there is my vision of loveliness."

Tall and broad of stature, with grey mutton-chop whiskers adorning his face, Sir Hugh looked more like a publican than a doctor or a scientist. Hannah suspected he could hide a number of his mice within his enormous sideburns. Thick-corded arms should have carried kegs of beer, and his large hands seemed entirely unsuited to wielding a scalpel with delicate accuracy. Yet he was the country's most esteemed surgeon.

Or had been, until 1814, when Sir Hugh and Lady Miles had returned from the war and shut themselves away in their secluded Westbourne Green home. There, the family devoted themselves to research.

While his face always wore a cheerful smile,

Hannah saw the deep sadness that dwelt in her father's warm gaze. A pain they both shared when their beloved Seraphina's heart had stopped. Sir Hugh had subsequently found a way to keep the Afflicted's condition under control, but it was so horrific that society was protected from any mention of it.

In this modern world, witches were no longer burned at the stake, but the mythical powers of a woman mage made the population nervous. In the rural community, curious eyes were deprived of the spectacle of Lady Miles, and Hannah could walk without the twitter of gossip following her footsteps. The tiny settlement had only five large houses, of which theirs was one. Seraphina had built the rambling, Gothic-inspired mansion when she became engaged to Sir Hugh. As her domain, Lady Miles had a tall, square turret with a dragon-adorned finial that pointed to the sky. With its panoramic views over the rural pastures, she conducted her own quiet research.

Into the earth Lady Miles had dug rooms for her beloved's laboratory. In the cool, windowless network of rooms he established a place of science, where he strove to advance man's knowledge of himself. Hannah could never make the moniker of *mad scientist* fit. His course was also hers and if he were mad, did that mean she likewise was addle-brained or insane?

"Stop daydreaming, Hannah, or we shall be late.

What is in the box?" Sir Hugh held out his arm to her.

She smiled in indulgence even as she wrapped her hand around his thick forearm. "We are supposed to be late, Papa. Nobody arrives on time. But if you insist on being terribly gauche and arriving early, at least I will be able to help Lizzie prepare for her grand entrance. As to the box, it contains Mother's surprise for the evening."

A broad smile crinkled the corners of his eyes. "I shall have to wait to see what Sera has constructed. You know the Loburns adore you, and I have much to discuss with the marquess. There has been some improvement in my mice and I believe we may be on the verge of a breakthrough at last."

Ah, there was the reason for his impatience—some news to carry to his patron. The marquess was head of the Society of Unnatural Scientific Study, a group of men who sought to pierce the veil of mystery around those people who defied God's laws. Hannah pitied the small creatures confined to their cages in laboratories around England. They did not know that they gave their lives to advance humankind.

The carriage conveyed them from the lush expanse of Westbourne Green, along Uxbridge Road, and toward the bustle of London. The farther they travelled into the city, the more the streets became crowded with horses, carriages, and pedestrians. Hannah breathed a sigh of relief upon seeing the congestion; it would delay their arrival.

They alighted at one of the most desirable addresses in England—Grosvenor Square, Mayfair. Tonight's was an exclusive affair. Only two hundred people would be present to celebrate the engagement of the daughter of the Marquess of Loburn to the Duke of Harden.

The marquess was both Sir Hugh's patron and his friend. Despite the taint of madness, magic, and death that pervaded their lives, her father provoked curiosity whenever he went out in public. The Afflicted might only be two per cent of the peers in London, but they represented a percentage with immense power and influence. Nobles demanded answers to the curse that had taken their wives, daughters, and sisters.

The *ton* expected a cure and Sir Hugh, along with his fellow SUSS scholars, were supposed to provide one. He fielded all questions with the good humour of a politician and wrapped his answers in nonsense and scientific babble, so that those asking never knew the cure still eluded him.

"Will you be all right on your own, my dear?" He patted Hannah's hand as they crossed the entry hall to the ballroom.

He fussed as though she were still a child frightened of being lost in a crowd, not a woman used to her own company. "Yes, Papa. You go find the marquess and I will offer my assistance to Lady Loburn before I go to Lizzie."

With some relief, Hannah found they were not, in fact, the very first to arrive. There were at least ten other people in the ballroom to save her from that awkwardness. Their hostess was easy to spot: a tall woman who bore an uncanny resemblance to a bird of prey. With an eagle eye, a hawk-like hook to her nose, and rapid motions, she could have been a caricature of herself, except that her avian appearance concealed a generous heart.

Whenever Hannah met Lady Loburn, she wondered how the lady's daughter had not inherited her looks from either her mother or her lean father. It was a matter that aroused Hannah's scientific curiosity, but good breeding kept her tongue silent.

"Lady Loburn." Hannah bobbed a curtsey. "I have the entertainment for tonight. My mother said not to open it until the exact moment arrives."

"Oh, brilliant. Thank you, Hannah." She took the box from Hannah and brushed a hand over the top.

"May I do anything to assist?" Hannah asked.

Her hostess reached out and patted her cheek. "My little angel of efficiency. Could you please ensure the housekeeper has everything in hand below stairs, and then run up and see how our Lizzie progresses?"

"Of course. I do wish to see Lizzie before the ball

commences. I have a letter for you from Mother." She extracted the letter and set it atop the box.

A warm smile softened Lady Loburn's sharp features. "Thank you. I do so look forward to news from Sera. I shall tuck this away to savour later, when I am alone."

With tasks allocated, Hannah headed back along the main corridor to the hidden servants' stair.

When her mother and father had been called to battle, the young Hannah was left in the care of Lady Loburn. She imagined an army camp preparing to meet the enemy looked a lot like the marquess's kitchens. Maids in starched white aprons and men in their fine livery marched back and forth. Serving trays and dishes were arrayed on the long table, waiting to be filled and carried upstairs. Orders were shouted and staff jumped to fulfil the demands.

She spotted the housekeeper in her black uniform. The efficient woman had everything in hand, down to the timing of the hors d'oeuvres and the correct temperature of the champagne for the celebratory toasts. Satisfied the evening would run smoothly, Hannah headed back up the stairs and knocked on the door of a second floor bedroom.

"Come in," someone said.

She pushed open the door into quite a different battlefield, the complete opposite of the ordered routine of the kitchens. Up here, chaos reigned. Women dashed back and forth, clutching clothing or accessories. The wardrobe doors hung open as though the piece of furniture had tried to fan itself in exhaustion. Drawers were half open, their contents draped over the sides. Even the bed was unmade, as though the occupant of the room had only recently arisen.

Three maids clustered around the dressing table with its large and ornate mirror. Their charge sat before it on a padded stool.

"Hannah!" Lizzie exclaimed from under all the attention. "Come tell me which earrings I should wear. We simply cannot decide."

Hannah bent down and kissed the air next to Lizzie's cheek and considered herself fortunate to have such a friend. Their mothers had been firm friends as girls and while one had married up and the other down, the two women had remained close. When they bore daughters at the same time, it seemed natural to continue the bonds of sisterhood to the next generation. When war intervened, Hannah had been raised under this roof with Lizzie; the two young women considered themselves sisters by friendship, rather than blood.

Hannah cast a critical eye over her best friend. Lizzie wore a pale pink silk gown with silver embroidery that offset her delicate complexion and blonde hair. The long curls were wound up on her head. A three-strap headpiece embellished with pearls kept the mountain of hair in place.

Next, she studied the fortune in jewellery scattered over the dressing table's surface. Rubies, diamonds, and emeralds were tossed down as though they had been made of paper or paste. Hannah frowned. What were they thinking, trying to match a coloured gem to pink—to say nothing of her friend's fair colouring? It would never do for her to clash with her earrings and necklace on such an important night.

"The diamonds. The colour won't detract from your ensemble, but the sparkle will add to the effect." She picked up the long drop earrings and handed them to the maid.

She watched to make sure her friend's evening was perfect. "Your mother sent me to make sure you would be suitably late to go down."

Lizzie laughed. "But how can I keep my darling Francis waiting? How I long to dance with him and feel his arms around me."

Hannah waggled a finger in Lizzie's face. "Don't even think of being early. As a future duchess, you would spark a trend. You simply cannot have people arriving on your doorstep early. It won't do."

Lizzie shooed away the maids and rose. She was exactly the right height, with a plump bosom, enviable curves, and the alabaster skin of a woman who never encountered sunlight. Coupled with blonde hair and vivid blue eyes, Lizzie was the storybook beauty.

By comparison, Hannah's brown hair and brown eyes allowed her to practically blend into the wood panelling, and she was too tall and flat-chested to ever attract the glances her friend's form elicited.

Lizzie took her hands and a rare serious glint entered her gaze. "I cannot believe that I will soon be an old married woman."

"It is no mystery to me. You have been inundated with suitors ever since you came out." Hannah had watched the whirlwind of Lizzie's debut. For three years she had considered her options. Many late nights had been spent in this bedroom discussing the merits of each suitor, but only one had captured her heart.

"If only we could find a suitable match for you." Lizzie frowned and then chewed her lip. "I swear, as duchess it will be my first task to see you wed. Then we'll have children to raise together, just as we were."

Hannah shook their clasped hands and stopped her friend from a review of her discarded suitors. "Don't, Lizzie. You know I have no desire to marry. Do not torment me so."

The Fates had decreed she would walk a lonely path, but she didn't want her sad state to remove some of the shine from Lizzie's evening. Nothing should spoil her grand engagement party.

"At least, dear Hannah, do say you will consider being my companion once I am wed? I cannot imagine embarking on married life without you by my side. Who else will I discuss all the horrid details of my wedding night with?" Lizzie winked.

Hannah laughed. "But you could not possibly tell me tales of your wedded passion. It wouldn't be seemly."

"I don't give a fig for seemly. Promise we are sisters forever? I cannot live without your friendship." Lizzie held out her hand, pinkie finger extended.

Hannah drew a deep breath and smiled, then wrapped her pinkie finger around that of her friend. "I promise. When the day arrives that Mother and Father no longer need me, I shall devote myself to you and your family."

Yes, she was loved and wanted.

Just not in the way that a woman longed for.

# 2

As the evening, flowed, so did the champagne and the conversation. Hannah listened to the music and watched the dancers. There was comfort in being on the periphery of society. She could enjoy events as an observer without having the eyes of everyone upon her. In that regard she pitied the newly engaged woman, as every aspect of her person was minutely scrutinised. It reminded her of the samples her father placed on glass and peered at under his microscope.

Yet Elizabeth shone all the brighter with the attention and outsparkled the diamonds at her throat and earlobes. She took to the floor with her duke and everyone remarked upon how elegant and attractive they were as a couple. Francis Voss, the Duke of Harden, possessed the same blond colouring as his fiancée. While not a tall man, he had straight limbs and a finely hewn face with open, honest blue eyes. Overall, his countenance made women, both young and old, sigh as he passed.

Lizzie was besotted with her intended and would make a fine duchess. Hannah had no doubt her friend would mature into the sort of matron that others looked up to and sought out for her patronage.

Just watching them, it was obvious it was a love match and not one orchestrated by Lizzie's parents. The couple had eyes for no one but each other, and they could have been dancing alone and not in a crowded ballroom. The duke adored his fiancée and a pang shot through Hannah's chest. What would it be like, to have a man look at you like that and to know there was someone in the world who loved you in such a manner?

A dark shadow flowed across Hannah's line of sight and she blinked. A wraith stalked the edges of the ballroom, marring the happy atmosphere with a mist of gloom. A shiver ran over her skin and she wondered if the man was really there, or if it were a nightmare apparition conjured by a mage. Perhaps she should have asked her mother to set wards around the mansion to ensure no demons or foul magic ruined the evening.

"I see Viscount Wycliff darkens our evening with his foul presence," the heavily veiled woman beside her whispered.

Hannah recognised the outline and voice of the

late Lady Albright. When her pulse had stopped, her husband had set her aside to subsist on the charity of others. Because noble ladies still walked among them, society had had to invent new rules to cope with the dead. The deceased Lady Albright was referred to as the *late* so as not to confuse her with the *current* Lady Albright.

"Who is he?" Hannah asked. She had never heard of the man, and was relieved that he was flesh and blood and not an evil spirit come to steal Lizzie's happiness.

The Afflicted woman leaned closer to Hannah and she caught the faint whiff of cloves, used to disguise the sweet rot that consumed her flesh. "Once, they were a fine family, but no more. His father was the worst kind of wastrel and money ran through his fingers as though it were water. Jonas Balfour is now the Viscount Wycliff but lacks any fortune to sustain the title."

"A fortune is not the only thing he lacks," a matron in puce silk interjected. "Manners also escape him. With his abominable rudeness, he scared off the only prospects who might have allowed him to rebuild his estate. His only hope now is to find some oblivious woman who is equally rude, like a title-hunting American heiress."

The women murmured agreement and then fell silent as a black gaze swept over them. Had he heard them from across the room? Impossible.

Hannah looked away, choosing instead to study a floral arrangement on the side table next to her chair. She counted herself fortunate that she was not the sort of woman to blush, but why didn't the viscount look away? She wanted a man to look at her with a heated stare, not one that seemed filled with scorn and, from the way his brows had drawn together, disapproval.

"Hannah, there you are." Lady Loburn swooped in, like the hawk who had spotted the mouse hiding in the long grass. "Would you fetch your mother's surprise from the marquess's study for me? I left it just inside the door."

"Of course." Hannah was relieved to escape the ballroom and the dark presence who absorbed all happiness with a look.

As she passed through the assembly, she brushed by the group clustered around Lord Albright and the *current* Lady Albright. Glances were cast toward the black veiled form of his previous wife, still talking to the other matrons. Hannah hoped there wasn't going to be a scene. Society loved to feast on the spectacle when the legally widowed lord paraded his young wife in front of his deceased, but still ambulatory, former wife.

The marquess's study was not far from the ballroom and Hannah headed along the hallway toward the front of the house. As she passed the parlour door, a sob caught her attention. She peered through the open door and saw a young woman sitting on a chaise, her shoulders heaving as she wept.

Unable to walk by a woman in distress, Hannah stepped inside. "Miss? Is everything all right?"

The woman raised her head and wiped tears from her cheek with the back of her hand. She was of an age similar to Hannah's, with dark brown curls that bobbed around her face. Sad brown eyes reminded Hannah of a shivering puppy she'd once seen on the street.

"Yes. Thank you. I foolishly spilled red wine on my dress and it is quite ruined." She picked at a series of red marks on her pale green gown.

Hannah squinted at the splatter. It didn't look like red wine, but something darker and thicker. Like tomato soup, but she was certain no such course had been served this evening. "Would you like me to fetch a maid? We might be able to clean it off."

"Oh. No. I don't want to be any bother. Silly to cry over a dress, I know, but it's new." Her hands scrunched the fabric and the stain disappeared within the folds.

Hannah well understood the despair of ruining a new gown, especially among those who seldom had the extra coin to keep abreast of fashion. She had stayed away from any food on the buffet that might have dribbled onto hers. "If you are sure you do not require assistance, I do have an errand to run for the marchioness."

The other woman rose from the sofa. "I'll go back to the party. I'm sure no one will notice the mark but me."

Hannah followed the woman out and then turned in the opposite direction to continue on to the marquess's study. The wooden box sat on a sideboard just inside the door. She longed to know what her mother had created to mark Lizzie's engagement, but could wait a few more minutes for her curiosity to be sated.

With the box clutched to her middle, Hannah hurried back to the ballroom. She hummed to the music, but a chord froze in her mouth at the sight of the cool blonde by the double doors. A vivid blue dress clung to her form and revealed the swell of her bosom. A tall man with dark hair rested one arm on the wall by her head. Hannah didn't recognise the man, but she did have the misfortune to be acquainted with the young woman.

The man glanced at Hannah and then leaned down to whisper in the woman's ear.

A throaty laugh mingled with the music from within. "Oh, that is no one important. Only Miss Hannah Miles fetching and carrying, as her sort should."

"I do hope you are having a pleasant evening, Lady Gabriella," Hannah murmured, and ignored the noblewoman's barb. She was only making sport for her latest beau.

Hannah stood at the top of the ballroom stairs and surveyed the crowd. She spotted Lady Loburn now in a cluster around the happy couple. Sir Hugh stood in the entrance to the billiards room talking to a group of men, no doubt explaining to them all how his research advanced. The upper echelon were keenly interested in whether he had identified a cure, wanting their wives and daughters retrieved from death's clutches. Men who had already remarried, such as Lord Albright, were less keen on a cure.

Viscount Wycliff circled the outer edge of the group, like a shark about to dive through a school of fish. What interest had he in her father's work? Perhaps an Afflicted sister or cousin? How odd that the men all kept their backs to the nobleman. Every one declined to acknowledge his presence in a public snub. In that case, why had the man been invited at all? She would have to ask Lizzie the reason later.

He glanced up and in her direction. Hannah gripped the box more tightly and concentrated on the stairs beneath her feet. It wouldn't do to fall and tumble the box to the floor. She made her way toward the evening's hostess and caught the lady's eye.

"Perfect timing, Hannah. Come along." Lady Loburn took Lizzie's hand and that of the duke and led them out on the dance floor. She said nothing, but simply waited for the crowd to fall silent.

Anticipation raced around the room as people shuffled toward the walls, leaving the four of them alone in the centre. Elizabeth rested her hand on the duke's arm and her eyes sparkled with happiness. Hannah held the box and reassured herself that everyone was looking at Lizzie, not at her.

When Lady Loburn held the attention of everyone present, she spoke. "We have gathered tonight to celebrate the engagement of Lady Elizabeth to his grace, the Duke of Harden. To mark this occasion I have a special surprise. A gift created by the mage, Lady Seraphina Miles."

Lady Loburn gestured to Hannah. Taking her cue, Hannah set the nondescript box on the floor and undid the brass catch. Then she flicked the lid open and stepped back. Her mother had not whispered a single word about the gift and Hannah had not a clue to prepare her for what might emerge. It could be a unicorn or a troop of dancing mermaids.

At first nothing happened, although Hannah suspected her mother had given the enchantment a delay, to allow her time to move away from the box. Then a faint light glimmered, as though the box contained a lit candle, and the flame waved back and forth. The small light expanded until white radiance spilled over the top of the box.

The light grew into a pillar rising from the small box. It reached two feet, then four, and soon it was six feet tall and still reaching toward the ceiling like a magic beanstalk in a fairy tale. As the shaft of light grew, the candles in the ballroom dimmed until the room was in darkness except for the glow from the enchantment.

A murmur ran through the crowd as the luminescent shape continued to climb until it brushed the ceiling. Then the column began to pulse and hum. A few seconds passed, then it exploded, to a surprised gasp from everyone present. As though it were made of glass, the pillar shattered into thousands of pieces that flew outward. Women cringed and men held up their arms to ward off the shards, but before the slivers could reach anyone, they transformed into glittering butterflies.

Cries of wonder arose from those assembled as crystal butterflies circled the room. As they flew, their wings emitted a musical refrain. With each beat, they caught and refracted light and sent rainbows spinning in every direction. Twice around the room they swooped. Then they turned like a flock of birds and descended on the engaged couple.

Lizzie and her fiancé disappeared under a glittering curtain. Tinkling noises and giggles came from behind the living wall. Over a number of long moments, the butterflies reformed until the couple were clothed in the dazzling artificial insects. Lizzie wore a tiara and gown composed of butterfly gems. The duke wore a bespoke suit of tiny vibrating crystals, including one clinging to his cravat to become a stock pin.

The duke took Lizzie's hand and the two of them

experimented by taking a few steps. Murmurs of wonder came from the watchers as the butterflies swayed with the couple and their wings gave off a musical note to accompany the movement.

Emboldened by the experiment, Lizzie and the duke tried a few more dance steps. The crowd was captivated as the two danced to music created by their magical clothing. Draped in the sparkling butterflies who were also tiny musicians, they seemed ethereal—like fairy folk come to dazzle lesser mortals.

Hannah could only gape at the beautiful display. The newspapers would be filled with stories of the sight for weeks to come. Pride welled in her chest. Her mother had crafted the most beautiful engagement gift. What woman wouldn't want to be clothed in singing, jewelled butterflies?

The dance ended and the two players bowed to one another. As the last note faded, the butterflies once again took flight, leaving Lizzie and the duke in their fabric evening wear. As a flock, the butterflies rose up and hovered. They formed two entwined hearts that seemed composed of a thousand diamonds, and made everyone sigh.

Their display over, the butterflies rolled together into an enormous sphere and with a silent bang, they exploded and rained down upon the floor as tiny, sparkling confetti. Flakes covered Hannah's outstretched arms in shimmering scales and for a moment, she was part of the magic that had enveloped the couple.

The ballroom floor now resembled the ocean when the sunlight lights the waves and dusts the surface with gems. The candles relit themselves in the overhead chandeliers and wall sconces.

Lady Loburn drew a handkerchief from her bosom and dabbed at her eyes. "That was beautiful. Do tell Sera it was a most marvelous culmination of the evening."

"I shall tell Mother everything, Lady Loburn," Hannah said as she closed the box and picked it up.

Their hostess gestured to the musicians at the end of the room and the dancing continued, while Hannah returned to her place at the side, away from anyone's notice.

**3**

---

Perched on her chair, Hannah watched as men claimed partners for the country dance and escorted them to the floor. Her mother had wanted her to have two dances, but she had only managed a polka with her father, catching him on the way to the dining room. None of the men cast any glances in her direction.

With one exception.

A shiver worked down her spine.

She peered through the crowd and tried to find the late Lady Albright, but she could see no trace of the woman veiled in black. Odd that she wore mourning colours when she was the mourned. Perhaps she draped herself in black to mark the death of her marriage. The current Lady Albright laughed and smiled out on the dance floor. If the sight made

Hannah uncomfortable, she could only imagine how it hurt the displaced woman.

"She must have gone already," Hannah murmured into her glass of punch.

A violinist hit a sour note that screeched in a long, never-ending wail. Hannah winced, as did the dancers. Across the room, Lord Wycliff turned his penetrating stare to the performer responsible for the noise. Out on the parquet floor, the dancers made a misstep. The carefully orchestrated score turned chaotic as the musicians lost their way. Dancers missed their cues and a crisis was narrowly averted when they all halted before any of the couples crashed into each other.

Still the high-pitched wail continued, though the players had all silenced their instruments. Then Hannah placed the sound. It was no out-of-tune violin.

It was a woman screaming.

Then it ended abruptly.

Wycliff bolted from the room, shoving people out of his way. Gasps turned into louder remarks. "How rude!" The viscount was like a bloodhound on the trail of a fox and nothing would stand between him and the source of the cry.

All the other women in the room gathered to one side of the ballroom like herded sheep, their men standing guard. Women clasped hands, supported the distraught, and whispered among themselves.

Except Hannah.

She dropped her glass on a sideboard and wove her way through the immobilised dancers, her gaze locked on the direction Lord Wycliff had taken. He had gone to find what had prompted the scream, she was sure of it. On the way she met her father, emerging from the billiards room.

Sir Hugh reached out and squeezed her hand. "Stay here."

Hannah snorted under her breath at his two short and unnecessary words. She wasn't staying anywhere. Then he also disappeared. Hannah was either blessed or cursed with her mother's curiosity, a large dose of her father's intellect, and the stubbornness of both parents. She gave her father's broad back a head start and then brazenly disobeyed by following him.

Up the stairs, through the enormous archway of the ballroom, and down a darkened hallway she chased the last echo of the ear-piercing sound. When she came to an intersection in the corridor, she listened for the pounding footsteps of her father.

Two footmen approached her from the other end of the corridor, clumsily carrying a maid slumped between them. The prone woman's arms draped around their necks and each man had an arm hooked under her knees. One footman looked apologetic. How unseemly of them, he seemed to say, to carry an unconscious servant where any guest could see them.

Hannah guessed the woman was the source of the screaming and had fainted, which accounted for the blessed cessation of the high-pitched sound. It was a wonder it hadn't set off all the neighbourhood dogs.

"Is she unharmed?" Hannah asked, scanning the unconscious woman for visible injuries.

"Yes, Miss Miles. Just out cold," one of the footmen answered.

Being familiar with the house, Hannah prised open a section of panelling to reveal the servants' narrower hall beyond. "Good. Take her below stairs to revive, before anyone else sees you."

"Thank you, Miss Miles," he said as they passed through the aperture to return to their world below.

Farther down the corridor, men loitered in a doorway. Hannah edged closer to peer around them. Within, all was in darkness, save one bright point of light from the sole candelabrum on a desk. The long silver arms seemed out of place, better suited to a large table, and looked as though someone had hastily set it down.

A footman moved around the room lighting candles in the wall sconces. The growing light revealed the feminine touches in the room, from the lace doilies on the backs of the chairs to the soft pink hue of the chintz. Hannah had spent many an hour at the desk in this room, writing letters Lady Loburn dictated while she reclined on the patterned chaise.

She had chased her father to the private study of the lady of the house.

As the footman moved with a lit taper, piece by piece the dark was pushed back and the full scene revealed. Light flared over the cause of the screaming. Lying prone on the expensive carpet was the outstretched body of a man. His hands reached for something beyond his grasp, his body clad in the maroon livery of the Loburn household.

If this was simply a collapsed footman discovered by the maid, why all the screaming?

Someone in front of Hannah gasped and shouldered her out of the way in his hurry to leave. He ran past her, making gagging noises, and disappeared into the greenery of potted ferns. Hannah filled the vacuum his body had left, affording her a better view of the tragedy.

An interesting smell wafted to her nostrils and she closed her eyes and drew a deep breath. Sweet and yet with a savoury hint, it made her mouth water and she swallowed, tasting the air. It reminded her of the hors d'oeuvres that had been served earlier in the evening—salmon with a delicate hint of zesty cucumber. But what was a footman doing in here with one of the platters?

Opening her eyes, she stared at the head of the deceased—for it was plain that he had left this world and was not merely unconscious. His head was no longer a neat oval, but collapsed in on one side, from his left ear to the top of his scalp and from front to back. A full quarter of his skull appeared to be missing. The scene had the appearance of a hungry child diving into a pie and wrenching apart the crust in its haste. The skull glistened where someone had broken the edges. The unfortunate's brains would have spilled forth over the Persian carpet, had they not been absent.

Hannah cast around for what might have caused such a terrible injury, and lighted on the metal globe of her ladyship's paperweight, discarded on the floor next to a piece of skull with dark hair still attached.

*Oh, no.* Hannah had seen such an injury before— two years ago. The mysterious malady that struck down some members of the *ton* produced a startling appetite in the Afflicted. Even as their pulses slowed and then stopped, they developed a craving for forbidden fruit.

Such was what it meant to be one of the unnaturally Afflicted.

A hideous, gnawing hunger for brains.

It was a side effect that very few knew. Hannah was privy to the information because of her work with her father, and her mother's Afflicted state. When Sir Hugh and Lady Miles determined that some of the *ton* had been stricken with the same curse that had killed her, they were able to prepare for the inevitable craving. Sir Hugh sought out illegal resurrectionists in order to have enough slivers of brain on hand to feed each woman as she turned. All the while, he worked tirelessly to convince the Prince Regent and the Prime Minister of what would need to be done.

It had taken two gruesome murders like the one laid out before Hannah now to finally galvanise those in power into action. A new business arose, providing the Afflicted with "pickled cauliflower," specially treated to ease their symptoms.

The general population heard only rumours and panic had been prevented by a typhus outbreak that killed hundreds of Londoners. The status of the Afflicted further shielded them. When you were related to politicians and peers at the highest level, you were treated differently and had access to ways to silence the tongues of gossips. The people on the street were too worried about dying from over-crowding and poor sanitation to pay any attention to what happened in the dining rooms of the toffs.

Without the necessary sustenance, the bodies of the Afflicted deteriorated and they rotted in their expensive silken shoes. Regular consumption allowed them to heal their own wounds to some extent, but if rot set in too deeply, nothing save the removal of the limb would halt its progress.

Hannah wondered what had provoked the death of the footman. Had one of the unfortunate ladies in attendance succumbed to her frenzied hunger? Hannah could think of no other explanation for why the man's brain was missing from his skull. The Afflicted had their appetites, but if they all started simply taking what they required from unsuspecting Londoners, the city would descend into terrified chaos within a day.

The general population of England was kept in the dark about the exact nature of the disease that had stricken a small percentage of upper-class women. Just as many men worked hard to ensure the public stayed in a state of blessed ignorance through every means at their disposal.

Sir Hugh knelt next to the victim and his broad back broke Hannah's fixation on the missing brain matter. Only then did she notice the other occupant of the room. The dark shadow lit by candlelight only emphasised his resemblance to the Grim Reaper, bent over the slain man as though he were there to harvest his soul.

Lord Wycliff looked up as though he had sensed her regard and scowled in her direction. His expression was unreadable apart from a general sense of disapproval. No doubt women were not meant to be in the presence of death, but Hannah handled it often in her work alongside her father.

She shook her head and took a step backwards. There was nothing she could do here. Her help would be needed in the ballroom to quell the panic that would arise in the rest of the guests. The maid who had discovered the crime and raised the alarm with her screaming would prompt questions that would need smoothing over. Such matters never stayed below stairs. Indeed, servants were the mechanism by which gossip spread from household to household. Like fire, the more scandalous tidbits raced upstairs.

Hannah found Lady Loburn at the end of the hallway as though she dared not approach, even though it was her most private sanctuary that had been violated. The woman kept clasping and unclasping her hands, like a bird trying to find the right spot on its perch.

"What news, Hannah?" Her gaze narrowed to the avian stare.

Hannah glanced around to be sure no one would overhear her. "A most heinous crime, I am afraid. It seems one of the maids discovered a footman's body on the floor in your study, and from what I could discern, he has been murdered."

Lady Loburn gasped, one hand flying to her mouth even as she uttered a muffled, "No. Not under our roof, and certainly not *tonight*. This will ruin Elizabeth's evening, and it was all going so splendidly."

Hannah took the older woman's hand and drew her back toward the ballroom. "Shall we ask the musicians to play another tune? I'm sure a waltz will distract everyone from the terrible screaming. And perhaps more champagne for the guests? It will soon be time for the final toasts."

Lady Loburn squeezed Hannah's hand. "Yes. You are quite right. Let us organise a distraction while the men deal with events."

Hannah busied herself with ensuring that the evening recovered from the unexpected intrusion. She found the butler and asked him to keep everyone's glasses full while Lady Loburn instructed the musicians to resume their play.

Lizzie and her fiancé took the central position as the waltz struck up. Soon the source of the screaming became a whisper behind fans, until a man strode to the middle of the room and the revellers pulled back to give him space.

Tall and lean, Viscount Wycliff moved with the feline grace of a dancer, or a lethal fighter. Light on his feet and soundless, he glided over the parquet floor. He wore the darkest blue velvet coat, with a black waistcoat underneath. The candlelight picked out the subtle metallic embroidery of glinting navy. Raven-black hair was cropped short and dishevelled in the popular Brutus style. Although with this fellow, it looked as though it happened by nature rather than design, as he ran long fingers through his hair and further elongated the wild locks on top. His face was all sharp angles with slashes of black brows, his high cheekbones underscored by elongated sideburns and a square jaw.

Hannah shuddered. The wraith kept materialising before her like a reoccurring nightmare. While the viscount wasn't handsome, he was certainly striking. The sort of man you couldn't ignore—not because of his looks, but because his entire persona reached out and demanded your full attention.

His eyes were points of darkness, like peering into a bottomless well at night. He narrowed his gaze as he surveyed the assembled dancers. Only when he had turned full circle did he speak.

"This evening a man has been most savagely murdered in such a manner as is done by one of the undead who cannot control their hunger. The Afflicted among you will step forward and make your presence known."

Gasps ran around the room. To most people, the Afflicted were gentle and charitable women, not depraved murderers. To point a finger at one as being a possible murderer was a heinous accusation. Women fanned their faces and stared at their neighbours. A woman with a white muslin veil over her face stepped back into the crowd, to be swallowed protectively by those on either side.

Hannah closed her eyes for a moment to centre herself. What right did this man have to ruin Elizabeth's ball? The matter should have been dealt with in private and behind closed doors, not shouted into a ballroom to distress everyone.

"This is uncalled for." One chap stepped

forward. "Leave the women be. They have suffered enough."

The black gaze swung to the challenger. He cocked his head, like a lion inspecting an insect that crawled over its paw. "Because they are dead you think they should be excused any crime? Tell me, who would remove the brain of a living, healthy man if not one of the cursed Afflicted?"

Hannah had already asked herself that question, and it unsettled her to share as much as a thought with the brooding viscount.

# 4

Women gasped. Another swooned and only the quick actions of her companion saved her before she hit the hard floor. A few men wobbled on their feet before grabbing hold of strategically placed chairs to balance themselves.

"Steady on!" someone yelled from the back of the room. "There is no need for such vulgar descriptions with ladies present."

"But how many of these ladies are Afflicted? Shall we number them?" Wycliff murmured. He cast his eyes downward, as though contemplating the intricate pattern made by the myriad tiny strips of wood under his feet.

When he looked up, his midnight gaze bored straight into Hannah, as though he expected her to turn traitor to her sex and point out who among the women had no pulse. She did the calculations in her head. Approximately two to three percent of the *ton* were Afflicted. With two hundred people present at the ball, that meant possibly four to six Afflicted among them.

The Marquess of Loburn moved to the centre of the floor and squared off against Wycliff. "You will remove yourself, Wycliff. You have no authority to humiliate the unfortunate women among us with your outrageous accusations. Quite frankly, I'm surprised you were invited this evening."

One black eyebrow arched. "I have a newly established authority in matters concerning Unnaturals."

Loburn did not move as he protected those under his roof. "Not that I recognise. The magistrate has been called and the matter is now in his hands. Given the victim was a footman, it is probably some unfortunate domestic matter or a gambling debt. We don't need you spreading lies."

Wycliff drew himself up and it seemed every person in the room held their breath, waiting to see what would happen.

"I shall return with the relevant authority to extract the names of the Afflicted you harbour." With that, he turned on his heel and stalked across the ball-room and up the stairs.

As his shadow was swallowed in the corridor, those present exhaled a collective sigh. Conversation rose and fell around the room as the murder and call to unmask the Afflicted was discussed. Hannah dodged around the huddled groups as she sought out her father.

"I think now might be the time for us to retire. There is nothing more we can do here, and morning is not far off." He drew her back to the entrance and asked a footman to have their carriage brought around.

"What of the body? If an Afflicted did indeed remove the footman's brain, then he will rise in a few days as a secondary Afflicted," Hannah whispered her words, cautious that no one overhear them.

She remembered the horrifying discovery they made when the Affliction had first struck. Two innocents had been murdered by family members who were driven mad by their condition. The victims in turn rose from their coffins with a ravenous and uncontrollable hunger. Those creatures, lacking their minds, were things to fuel nightmares. Mages, politicians, and high-ranking peers worked hard to protect England from such a terrible plague.

Sir Hugh glanced around, confirming no ears listened to their secrets. "We will give his family time to grieve first, then we shall ensure he does not rise. The marquess knows what must be done."

Satisfied, Hannah allowed herself to be helped up into the carriage. On their way home, she rested her cheek against the worn fabric of the seat and closed her eyes. Her mind was in turmoil as she sorted through events of the evening...and the dark eyes that had drilled through her. With only a look, Lord Wycliff had stripped away her protective layers as though he saw all her flaws, naked and exposed.

The sway of the carriage lulled her and she drifted in a half sleep. The world had changed since Napoleon's defeat the previous year, bound in chains of dark magic and imprisoned beyond the reach of his mages. Victorious Englishmen came home, but for some officers their celebrations were cut short to discover their aristocratic wives or sisters had fallen ill and expired.

Lady Miles had been one of the first to die abroad. She had wielded her power for England on the Peninsula when she and two of her companions succumbed. At first it was assumed to be some French plot to assassinate the powerful English mage. Only the passage of time had revealed the true extent of the disease.

Hannah's mother and the others continued to deteriorate, even as their husbands fought on to push back the French. Then, in 1814, the French planned to unleash their plague on English soil. Through the actions of an English agent, the spread of the cursed face powder was limited to a few noblewomen in London.

Society couldn't afford to ostracise women in such high places, so the rules adapted.

These days, there were three expectations of a young lady of breeding.

She should be accomplished in at least one of the arts.

She should be decorous at all times.

She should never reveal the true state of her decay.

Society was built upon appearances and the sufferers engaged a number of tricks to hide the rot that consumed them from the inside. Heavy powder was one. A fan in constant use, another. A veil, as though in mourning, for those beyond a light repair. The wealthiest used a fine porcelain mask to trick the eye into seeing unblemished skin.

These unfortunate women were known as the Afflicted. A handful of women at Lizzie's engagement party had been victims of the Unnatural plague. Hannah knew some, for they visited her father heavily veiled, hoping he had some advance to reverse the damage. To think one of them might have been capable of such a brutal murder sent a shiver down her spine. How uncouth.

The jolt of the carriage stopping jerked her full awake and her father took her hand to help her down. As they climbed the steps to their Westbourne Green home, Hannah paused under the fading moonlight. The water in the nearby canal burbled as it flowed past one side of their property, cutting them off from their neighbours as effectively as a moat.

"Do you think it was one of them?" she asked.

Sir Hugh looked up, his gaze tracking a star, or perhaps simply a moth drawn by the lamp shining beside their front door. "Yes. Poor fellow had his brains completely removed and there's no sign of them. If it wasn't an Afflicted woman who is now a danger to society, then it was someone who wanted us to believe it was one of them."

Hannah tried to clear the mist gathering in her mind. Her fuddled thoughts were simply the result of a tiring evening. Yet all she could see was a pair of midnight eyes, piercing her soul and demanding to know her secrets.

THE NEXT MORNING, Wycliff stood before his superior to seek a warrant to serve on the Marquess of Loburn. In his time in the army, General Sir Manly Powers had been responsible for the formation of the Highland Wolves, a regiment of lycanthropes. His military position had turned into a civilian one after the war; he had been chosen recently by Parliament to spearhead the new Ministry of Unnaturals.

As Wycliff outlined the events of the night before, a look of incredulity rolled over Sir Manly's face that had nothing to do with the unseemly demise of a footman. "You asked Afflicted women to reveal themselves? In public? What were you thinking, man?"

Wycliff kept his hands clasped in the small of his back as he stood at ease before his commanding officer. He locked his frustration deep inside. His reasoning should have been obvious. "Given that the nature of the crime pointed to a particular type of perpetrator, I thought to narrow down the possible suspects with all dispatch, sir."

Sir Manly snorted. "This is why no one likes you, Wycliff—you're too damned impertinent."

At least a soldier always knew where he stood with Sir Manly; there was no mollycoddling. Wycliff was well aware of society's opinion of him and he had no intention of tugging his forelock and being obsequious to earn a pat on the head like a good boy.

The general dipped his quill in the ink pot and wrote a few lines in a bold, sweeping hand, then added a dollop of wax into which he pressed his seal. "Find a sensible woman to accompany you when you interview the ladies. Can't have you upsetting delicate constitutions more than you have already."

It took all his control not to burst out that the very idea was ridiculous. "They are dead, sir. I fail to see how I could *upset* them further than death already has."

"You will mind your manners around noble ladies and find a woman to act as chaperone. Am I understood?" Sir Manly dangled the warrant just beyond his reach.

It would seem that to achieve his objective, he would have to find a pliable woman to deposit in a corner and steadfastly ignore. "I understand perfectly, sir."

Warrant in hand, Wycliff rapped on the Marquess of Loburn's front door at the ungodly hour of ten o'clock. He didn't care. Last night he had caught Sir Hugh's whispered *not again* and ferreted the truth out of him. A murder had been committed by one of the foul Afflicted and he intended to find out who and bring them to justice.

The butler showed him into a parlour, where he prowled in front of the cold fireplace. Waiting. This was his life. His title opened doors, but he often found the rooms beyond deserted, the occupants having beat a hasty retreat out another exit. He was the undesirable, often left waiting in corridors or neglected rooms.

Society had judged him based on rumours and assumptions and then cast him aside. They expected him to scurry away like a chastised child, but he would not go quietly into the night. He was not so easily dissuaded that he would give up and go home with his tail between his legs. Those men didn't appreciate the extent of his patience. War had taught him the value of waiting.

He pulled a small volume from his jacket pocket, perched on a chair, and read.

It was two hours before Loburn appeared.

"Do you know what blasted hour it is?" the marquess demanded as soon as he entered the parlour.

A rhetorical question, since the clock was chiming twelve. Wycliff stood and tucked his book back into his pocket. His movements were slow, almost exaggerated. A small gesture that allowed him, in turn, to keep the marquess waiting, although for mere seconds and not hours. Only then did he bow. "I believe it is exactly ten hours after a footman was murdered under your roof by one of the Afflicted."

The older man rocked back on his heels. "You don't know that."

"No. But the circumstantial evidence is rather compelling, is it not?" Wycliff brushed the sleeves of his black jacket and tried not to care that he was unwelcome in this house. Not that any household greeted him with open arms, except the brothels, and they were most pleased to see his purse, not his person.

Loburn tucked his hands behind his back and, standing, denied Wycliff the basest civility of a seat. "Regardless, you're wasting your time here. The magistrate has the matter in hand."

"The magistrate was this morning directed to

hand the matter over to me." He reached into a different pocket and produced a folded sheet of paper. "This is my warrant from General Sir Manly Powers, authorising me to investigate all matters that involve an Unnatural creature."

Loburn snatched the paper and held it at arm's length. "You're working for the Ministry of Unnaturals? I never thought that would make it past Prinny."

"The Prince Regent specifically tasked us to deal with these creatures loose in England. I am the first investigator, and I report to the general. Who, as you see, has the power to remove this matter from the hands of the magistrate. I am directed to uncover the *person* responsible for the murder committed here." He couldn't stop his upper lip from curling back as he muttered the word *person*. The idea of what some women had become was distasteful and his tongue was reluctant to form the word. They were little better than walking corpses, but because they had titles and fortunes, they escaped the grave. Perhaps they would be better employed in the medical schools, advancing mankind's knowledge of anatomy.

"What do you want?" Loburn returned the paper and walked to a chaise. He flicked out the tails of his jacket and sat, but left Wycliff standing like a new recruit in the army. Another subtle signal that he was unwanted.

The warrant was carefully folded and tucked

away. "You will provide the guest list of all those in attendance last night."

Loburn gave a snort. "No."

Wycliff clenched his hands together behind his back. The prick of his nails in his palms gave him a focus point with which to control his temper. He needed to extract the list from Loburn and flying into a rage would achieve nothing, even if it would make him feel better about the way society treated him. "I need to identify which women present are lacking a pulse, so I may begin my enquiries."

"I'll not have you interrogating our fellow nobles in your rude and obnoxious manner and stirring up unnecessary trouble."

That was uncomfortably close to what Sir Manly had said earlier. Where would Wycliff procure a woman to stand as chaperone while he asked his questions?

The standoff was averted when the door opened and Lady Loburn entered wearing a pale blue morning robe with ermine trim.

Wycliff bowed and murmured, "Lady Loburn."

"What do you think, my dear?" Loburn said to his wife. "Wycliff has demanded all the ladies' names so he can question them."

She moved to her husband, who stood and took her hand. "Most certainly not."

"My thoughts exactly." The marquess stood a little taller now that his wife had taken his side.

"He cannot do that on his own. He does have a reputation for being blunt," Lady Loburn said.

Her husband frowned. "You think he should have access to our guest list?"

Wycliff was going to jump in, wave his warrant, and demand the information, but for once, he might achieve his goal by letting events play out.

The lady's piercing gaze fixed on Wycliff. "A crime has been committed in our home and the perpetrator must be found. It would have upstaged Lizzie's engagement in the papers today if Lady Miles had not worked her magic while the marquess greased a few palms. Obviously, we cannot have Lord Wycliff terrifying delicate ladies of our acquaintance. I would, however, trust Miss Hannah Miles to ask discreet questions on his behalf."

"What?" two men said in unison.

Now Wycliff frowned. The conversation had taken an unexpected detour, but it might neatly solve his problem. He just didn't want to leap at the offer like an untrained pup. He must put up some resistance to the idea first. "There is no need to involve anyone else in this enquiry, particularly not a woman."

Lady Loburn fixed him with an unwavering stare. "Miss Miles is the soul of discretion and she is known to our circle. Her presence will reassure those you intend to interview."

Wycliff's anger began to crawl its way back up

his chest. Why did society insist on treating him like a child in leading strings who needed a governess to restrain him? "This matter is not appropriate for a young lady of quality."

"Hannah is the daughter of Sir Hugh Miles, the doctor who is devoted to finding a cure for the Afflicted curse. She is her father's assistant and as such, has a unique insight into those you suspect of this crime." A faint smile pulled at Lady Loburn's thin lips.

Wycliff rubbed his chin as he considered the idea. He knew of Sir Hugh's reputation. His wife had been one of the first known Afflicted and also a mage. If the daughter had some understanding or intelligence about the Afflicted, she might be of some assistance. It would also satisfy Sir Manly. Once his superiors were happy with his arrangements, he had only to scare the woman off so he could continue—alone—to investigate the crime.

"Very well, if that is your condition for handing over the list." He ground out the words, but they were said now.

Lady Loburn smiled, but it was a cold thing that made Wycliff suspect he had just been manipulated by the older woman. To what end? "Excellent. I suggest you visit Sir Hugh and ask Miss Miles to call and retrieve the list. I will draw up the names of all the women in attendance and have it waiting for her to collect."

That wasn't quite how he'd wanted matters to unfold, but for the sake of another few hours he would soon have exactly what he wanted. How hard would it be to convince one foolish chit to hand over the list?

**5**

---

The beautiful primrose yellow silk dress that Hannah had worn to the ball was hung over the top of her dressing screen. She couldn't bear to shut it away in her wardrobe just yet. She rose and as she dressed in a grey striped cotton dress, she touched the silk gown with a fingertip. What would it be like to wear such fine dresses every day?

Discarding the whimsical thought, she tied a tough canvas apron around her waist to protect her clothes while she assisted her father. It didn't matter whether it were man or mouse that secreted bodily fluids, they proved equally stubborn to lift from her clothing. She was too practically minded to be careless with her dresses, and it wasn't as though anyone apart from her parents or the staff would see the ugly apron.

Today was a rare occasion—they would perform an autopsy on a woman who had died from her Affliction, who, moreover, was actually dead and not sipping tea in a parlour in London. Although the Afflicted among the *ton* appeared lifeless with their dull complexions and lack of pulse, they still shopped in Bond Street and rode in Rotten Row, unlike this poor woman, who lay still and lifeless on the table.

"Who was she?" Hannah asked as she laid out her father's equipment: scalpels for flesh, a small hand saw for bone. An instrument to help crank open the chest cavity was lined up next to metal bowls waiting to receive internal organs.

Hannah pondered the deceased's life and what path she had walked that had brought her in the end to Sir Hugh's stone table. It was unusual for someone to fall victim at such a late date. No new infections had occurred since the initial outbreak two years ago. The original plague had burned through the upper echelons over a period of a few weeks and then subsided.

Investigation and her father's tireless work had uncovered the source of the infection—a very expensive face powder used to whiten the complexion. That was why it only affected a handful of men and no one from the lower classes. Constant blotting of the ladies' faces allowed the disease to seep into their skin. Or had they inhaled it with the fine powder?

While they had identified the means by which

some members of the *ton* had been infected, exactly how it worked and what dark magic animated the dead were questions her parents still strove to answer.

"In life, she was a woman who earned her way as a maid in the employ of a woman of the demimonde. Then she happened upon a container of contaminated powder." Sir Hugh eyed the equipment arrayed on the tray and picked up his favourite scalpel.

"I thought they had all been destroyed." Hannah folded the sheet down to the woman's waist, so her torso was exposed to the overhead lamps—candles with mirrors behind them to amplify the light they provided.

Once the connection had been made to the cause of the plague, the contaminated powder had been gathered up and burned, along with the two people responsible for selling the magical poison. Only the samples held by her father were spared. Those were kept locked in a safe. He wanted to discern what within the fine substance stilled the heart, yet kept the limbs and mind animated.

Sir Hugh looked up at his daughter and narrowed his gaze, as though trying to determine how much to say. "It would appear a gentleman purchased the powder as a gift for the courtesan two years ago. It sat unopened on her dressing table all this time, among numerous other gifts from her admirers. Eventually she moved rooms and in the tidy-up, the container was given to this lass, her loyal maid."

"A gift that was no gift at all, but a death sentence. But why did she die completely? Why has she not remained ambulatory?" The question worried at Hannah's mind. Why had the plague taken a different course in this woman? The Afflicted sickened and their pulses stopped, but they continued to go about their daily tasks.

"That is what we must try to discern. From what I understand, she continued to function for six months after her heart stilled. Then, last week, she simply fell down and didn't rise again. Perhaps the curse is altered by the age of the powder?" Sir Hugh sliced through the skin of the woman's torso with his scalpel and Hannah helped to peel it back, revealing the layer of muscle underneath.

"How did she feed? Perhaps this was a result of starvation?" Hannah asked.

"That is a possibility. Her former employer found her a new situation in the home of another Afflicted. She was fed in lieu of wages, but given the price of 'pickled cauliflower,' I suspect she teetered on the edge of starvation." Sir Hugh put down the scalpel and picked up a pair of long-handled shears, to snip the ribs.

A rap at the door drew their attention. The maid, Mary, hardly ever ventured down to the basement.

The staff preferred to stay clear of the place where death was asked to surrender her secrets. Hannah let go of the piece of flesh and wiped her hands on the apron before opening the door.

The maid kept her eyes fixed on Hannah's face, not daring to look farther into the examination room. "Gentleman here to see you, miss."

"Oh, not now," her father grumbled. He hated to be interrupted at his work.

The maid poked her head in a fraction. "Not you, sir—he's here to see Miss Hannah."

"Me?" Mary must have slipped and hit her head. What gentleman would call on her?

Mary's brown eyes widened. "Oh, yes, miss. Asked most specifically for Miss Hannah Miles."

Hannah glanced back at her father. He shrugged and then waved his shears, as though a gentleman caller were an everyday occurrence in their household. "Off you go, Hannah. Don't keep the gentleman waiting."

She took the stairs slowly while her mind raced, trying to determine who the caller could be. She had no gentlemen acquaintances. Perhaps it was a tradesman who wanted to discuss some household business? By the time she reached the parlour door on the first floor, she had convinced herself she would find the butcher within, wanting to discuss what cuts of meat the family would require next week.

Instead, she found the wraith.

Cloaked in black and midnight blue once again, he stood looking out the window at the front garden. He turned upon hearing her intake of breath. His nostrils flared as though she brought a distasteful aroma into the room. Or perhaps he didn't approve of the rural view out the window? His black gaze fixed her to the spot.

"Viscount Wycliff." She stared back, etiquette fled her mind in the moment of surprise. Under his glare she found even her ability to blink had deserted her, and she scrambled to think why he could be calling. No one from London society ever ventured voluntarily so far into the rural landscape—except for Elizabeth, on what she called her *expeditions*.

"Miss Miles." He bowed.

The act reminded her to drop a brief curtsey and gave her a chance to moisten her dry lips and gather her rampant thoughts.

He gestured to her apron. "I did not mean to interrupt your work."

Looking down, Hannah found a bloody smear where she had wiped her hands after handling the dead woman's flesh. No wonder he looked ready to snarl at her. What well-bred woman would greet a visitor in a bloodstained apron? For once she wished for her usual invisible state, so she could escape his piercing regard. "I do apologise, Lord Wycliff. I am assisting my father with a delicate procedure."

Her father had probably cracked the woman's ribs apart by now and would need help in weighing and assessing her internal organs. What information would they yield? Never before had one of the Afflicted been given to Sir Miles's autopsy table for study. They made do with rats and mice, or asked her mother to detail her experiences. Only when Hannah looked up did she realise the viscount was talking.

What had he been saying? "I'm so sorry, my lord, could you repeat that?"

His gaze narrowed and he blew out a sigh. It would appear he had little patience with women, particularly those who weren't paying attention. "I said, I require your assistance with the investigation of the murder committed last night. Lord and Lady Loburn will only entrust the guest list to you, and it has been suggested your assistance would settle some of the concerns of those involved."

"Oh." How odd. Why would Lord Loburn involve her?

He tapped one finger against the top hat in his hands. "I am investigating the matter and must ascertain which women in attendance last night are Afflicted. They must be interviewed about their movements during the ball." He continued to stare at her, as though he were a hawk deciding whether or not to pounce on the mouse.

"Oh."

Now he arched an eyebrow. He probably suspected her of being dim-witted.

She must expand her responses to more than a single syllable. "What manner of assistance do you require from me to...allay the concerns of those involved?"

"My superior at the Ministry and Lady Loburn both believe that propriety would be better served if you were present during the interviews. Although I completely understand if such unpleasantness is too much for you to bear." His voice dropped to a murmur. His hypnotic stare likewise lowered and released her from its grip.

Propriety aside, a murder investigation was no place for a gently bred woman. But if a woman was required to stand beside her noble kind, who better than one with another woman's blood staining her apron?

Hannah had her own reasons for wanting to discover the identity of the killer. The person responsible had placed a permanent stain on Lizzie's night. That was unforgivable. All the talk should have been of Lizzie's grand engagement, how ravishing she looked, and the magical surprise. Instead, tongues would wag about the horrific murder, and her mother and the marquess worked through the night to ensure the newspapers kept silent on that particular topic.

Not to mention the fact that her father would want to study a rogue Afflicted. What had driven the

Afflicted to such hunger that she'd broken open a man's skull with two hundred other people in the house? Would the desperation be curbed now that the offender had fed, or would she strike again in such a manner?

Hannah wiped her hands on her apron again, deliberately drawing Wycliff's gaze to the bloodstain. "I think I am strong enough to sit through a few interviews. I can fetch the list this afternoon, once I have finished my work in the laboratory."

He nodded and ground his jaw. An uncomfortable silence stretched between them, before he shoved his top hat onto his head, indicating he was leaving. "I will call again this evening, if that is permissible? I am most keen to further my investigation."

"Of course." Hannah made a note to remember to change clothes before he returned, and most definitely to wash her hands.

The maid showed their visitor out and Hannah returned to her father, trying to bring order to the turmoil Wycliff's presence wrought in her mind. She pushed through the heavy steel door to find her father well progressed in his grim task. The ribs were pulled open, like doors to a devotional cabinet that revealed the secret scene within.

Hannah peered at the empty stomach cavity. People were muted watercolours inside. "It was

Viscount Wycliff. He has asked for my assistance in the murder enquiry."

Sir Hugh frowned. "Odd chap, that one. But the person must be caught, especially if it is an Afflicted with a taste for footmen."

Which exactly summed up another of Hannah's reasons for agreeing to assist, even though her mind screamed a warning at having anything to do with the brooding man. The monster responsible must be stopped.

It was one thing for the Afflicted to find nourishment in the minds of the deceased, where the families of the latter were fully compensated for the organ removed, but it was another thing entirely to pluck the thoughts and feelings from the still living. Not to mention that such an act of violence passed on the Affliction to a new host, a fact they strove to keep a secret from all but the highest levels within Parliament and the military.

"Lord Wycliff does seem to dwell under a rather dark cloud." The viscount carried a foul mood with him, as though he raged at the world. And yet his piercing eyes triggered something deep inside Hannah. A warning that she should heed, mingled with a compulsion that meant she could not stay away from him.

Sir Hugh removed the woman's liver and waited while Hannah fetched a bowl to receive the organ. "War changes men. Some for the better. Others, like

Wycliff, become angry at the change thrust upon them."

"How did it change him?" What a strange thing to say. What metamorphosis had the viscount undergone? Or did some men see such horrors that they could never forget?

"A campaign on the Peninsula had a particularly ugly end. His entire regiment was slaughtered and, as the officer, he was held accountable. He was also the only survivor. Many thought he should have died with his soldiers. He took it hard."

Hannah took a breath, about to ask more questions, when her father fixed his warm gaze on her. "The exact details are his story to tell or not, Hannah. Do not think to go prying into other people's business."

He tapped the bowl containing the liver, reminding her that another would soon be needed. Hannah swallowed her questions, placed the bowl on the table, and fetched the next one.

"But that is exactly what I will be doing in aiding him—prying into the business of others." What questions would he ask, and who would he unmask as Afflicted? Many speculated on who was or wasn't Afflicted as though it were a ghoulish parlour game. Some were known, but others hid in plain sight. Should they suffer the consequences of being unmasked?

Sir Hugh cut the blood vessels that held the

kidneys in place. "You will be prying for entirely different reasons, Hannah. One would be to satisfy that curious mind of yours. The other is to bring a murderer to justice, and perhaps advance our knowledge about what drove the poor sufferer of this plague to take such tragic actions when we have not had any incidents for two years now."

There was one problem with curiosity—only feeding that hunger would settle it down. Hannah's questions about Lord Wycliff would not be so easily dismissed. Her finding out the man harboured some tragic history might make suffering his boorish company a little more bearable. Like the brooding hero of a gothic novel who bore terrible scars on his soul. Hannah would just need to construct a tolerable plot around him.

Father and daughter worked side by side all morning, until the woman on the table looked hollow. Her organs were arrayed in bowls after being weighed and measured. Next they would be preserved in alcohol for further study and analysis.

"Shall we look at her heart now? I saved it for last." Her father had the look of an excited child.

"Of course." Hannah handed him the rib cracker.

He opened the chest cavity further, exposing the last organ. Hannah gasped and held a hand to her mouth. The sweet odour of putrefaction overwhelmed them as the surrounding caul was pulled free. The heart was no lovely deep red thing, but green and rotten. The outer edges had turned black as it decayed in the woman's chest.

Sir Hugh hummed to himself as he worked. "How curious. None of the other internal organs show any sign of decay, consistent with the woman's dying just yesterday. Yet by the heart, one would think she died some time ago, when the original disease struck her down."

Rotten to the core, Hannah thought. Were all the Afflicted like this on the inside?

Sir Hugh looked up, as though he had heard her thoughts. "Don't tell your mother. No point in distressing her."

**6**

---

Hannah didn't only wash her hands when they finished up. She ordered a bath, stripped off her work clothes, and scrubbed every inch of skin she could reach. There was something about seeing the woman's heart rotting in her chest that clung to her, and no amount of pressure with the short-bristled brush could scrub the memory away.

Dressed once again, she tried to sweep the sight from her mind as she took the spiral staircase to her mother's tower.

After being advised of the murder on their return from the ball, Seraphina had worked through the night using magic to head off rumours of the gruesome murder and to give the people of London something else to talk about over breakfast.

"Come in."

"I have been waiting all day to talk to you, but didn't want to interrupt your work. Did you manage to silence the rumours?" Hannah crossed the floor to the square window.

Her mother sat in a wicker bath chair and watched birds circle over the fields. Hannah placed a kiss on a muslin-covered cheek and then took the armchair positioned next to the bath chair.

"I cannot silence wagging tongues, but I did release a more tantalising rumour for them to gobble up. I crafted the story that the Prince Regent has commissioned a gifted tailor to make him a new suit of clothes fashioned from cloth so sheer some think it invisible. Thrilled with the resulting outfit, he will promenade through the streets today. I set my little creature free a few hours ago to whisper at every door and window. The rumour of a gruesome murder cannot compete with the chance to see the Prince Regent in the altogether." As Lady Miles spoke, she turned her hands into wings that fluttered away from the tower.

"A shame it has taken the shine from Lizzie's evening." Hannah hardened her resolve to find the murderer who had sabotaged her friend's happiness with such a horrific event.

"Let us have no more talk of that. You need to tell me all about the ball and whether my gift was well received," Seraphina said.

Hannah couldn't describe the evening without leaping to her feet. She danced with an invisible partner as she told of Lizzie and the duke stealing everyone's breath when clothed in crystal butterflies. With events narrated and acted out, from the glorious moment when Elizabeth descended the stairs, to the entranced crowd that watched her magical butterflies, Hannah dropped back into the comfortable chair.

"I much prefer your poetic version of events. While I love your father dearly, he narrates as though he is reading from a textbook."

Hannah couldn't see the smile on her mother's face, but it infused her words and actions and she basked in the glow.

Seraphina clasped her hands together in her lap. "Let us move on to a more mysterious topic. Tell me of Viscount Wycliff and his visit here today."

"I do not think anyone could be poetic when describing the viscount. He strikes me as something one would find lurking in the pages of a horror story." Hannah told of his unexpected call and his strange request for her assistance.

"Keep your wits about you with that one, Hannah." Seraphina took Hannah's hand and placed it against her cheek.

"He expects me to act as chaperone while he questions the Afflicted who attended the ball last night. We know many of these women and there is not a murderer among them. What greater good is served by unmasking them unnecessarily?" Hannah had seen the crazed beings that could commit such a murder, and certainly no one had exhibited such behaviour at the ball. Viscount Wycliff must be mistaken. It must be a crime made to look as though an Afflicted were responsible.

Seraphina squeezed Hannah's hand. "Only you can balance a woman's privacy against the need to stop a killer, but I believe you will do the right thing when the time comes."

"Is there a way to use magic to discern the murderer's name? That would save many women from potential exposure." Magic touched so many aspects of their lives, you would think it would have a more practical purpose.

Seraphina sighed. "I am sorry—my power does not extend to the ability to read the human mind. That remains a mystery, even to me. Now be about your task, lest the viscount declare you tardy or worse, remiss."

Hannah worried all the way to Mayfair, and only the rapturous embrace of Lizzie relieved some of her concern.

"I have something scandalous to confide before Mother joins us." Lizzie took Hannah's hands and drew her toward the front parlour.

As she sat, Hannah remembered the young woman she had encountered in here, crying over the stain on her dress. Where had she gone last night? She couldn't recollect seeing her among the revellers, but then so much had happened.

Returning to the matter at hand, curiosity sparked in Hannah's mind. She couldn't imagine Lizzie doing anything more scandalous than taking two lumps of sugar in her tea instead of one. "Whatever have you done, Lizzie?"

Lizzie glanced around and pulled Hannah closer. Her voice dropped to a low whisper. "Out on the balcony last night, Francis kissed me. A proper kiss, too, and not a quick one stolen when the chaperone wasn't looking."

"Oh, Lizzie. Was it marvellous?" Hannah wanted to interrogate her friend. She had never been kissed, and probably never would. Secondhand information must sustain her.

*Just like secondhand love,* the tiny voice in the back of her head whispered.

Lizzie's blue eyes shone like a clear summer's day. "Yes. My knees went quite weak and only his strong arms around me kept me from swooning."

At that point Lady Loburn arrived and Hannah was deprived of her chance to bombard Lizzie with questions. That was something to tuck away for another time. Perhaps the night before her wedding, when Hannah would stay over and the two young ladies would talk all through the dark hours.

Lady Loburn had the list that Viscount Wycliff

sought, but Hannah decided to whittle his selection further. Of the two hundred people in attendance, the names of one hundred women had been written out in a neat hand. The three women worked all afternoon to reduce it further, a novelty for Lizzie and Lady Loburn.

"If I might enquire, Lady Loburn, how is Viscount Wycliff acquainted with the family that he was invited last night?" After two cups of tea, Hannah had worked up the courage to ask the question nibbling at her mind.

"Ah." Lady Loburn set down her quill and paused. She rapped a finger on the desk as she gathered her thoughts. "Yes, he was an odd addition, and no acquaintance of ours. You will have to ask your mother her reasons. Sera made a special request to have him added to the guest list."

"Mother? But she does not know him." Hannah reviewed her conversations with her mother and nowhere had she offered any hint of an acquaintance with the viscount. What was her mother up to?

Lady Loburn smiled at Hannah. "I have learned over the years not to question your mother when she makes strange requests. There is always a reason buried in them somewhere, even if it is not visible to the rest of us."

Hannah would ask her mother to explain her reason the next time they were alone. Had some premonition compelled her to interject the viscount into the proceedings? Hannah struggled to imagine how her mother thought that could be beneficial. If the man had been absent, the whole murder would have been dealt with quietly and not shouted about in the middle of the ballroom.

The women returned to discussing each name on the list and by early evening, Hannah was satisfied with the notations made. She said her goodbyes and returned home, where she and her father dined early. Her mother was ensconced in the tower and did not wish to be disturbed. Perhaps she didn't want to explain her actions to her daughter. Hannah would wait and would not be dissuaded from learning the truth.

Sir Hugh rose from the table to return to his laboratory. "Do you want me to stay, my dear, or can you handle the viscount on your own?"

Her father was fascinated by the rotten heart. He wanted to dissect it and try to force it to reveal the secret it held. Hannah folded her napkin. Propriety demanded a chaperone be present when a gentleman caller came to visit, but did the rules apply in such a situation? This was no suitor, nor was Hannah of any import to society. This was more akin to a business arrangement.

"We are discussing the guest list from last night. I do not believe we will require your supervision and the heart will not wait." The sad, neglected organ had been falling apart before they even removed it from the woman's chest. It would be unusable in another day and even alcohol would fail to preserve it.

Could her own heart break down in a similar fashion inside her body from lack of use?

Hannah adjourned to the front parlour and tried to settle with a book, but her mind had no intention of being stilled. It ranged over steep hills and climbed boulders as she chased random thoughts. Hannah might have been sitting for minutes or hours, when Mary coughed discreetly behind her hand.

"Lord Wycliff, miss." The maid beat a hasty retreat, relinquishing her position at the parlour door to the unstoppable force beyond.

Wycliff swept in the room like a storm cloud about to unleash lightning. "You have the list?"

The impertinent man hadn't even removed his hat. Hannah set the book aside and rose. She bobbed a brief curtsey, even if he had forgotten his manners. Did that make up for earlier in the day, when she had been the one who was remiss?

He snorted and gave the scantest bow, his gaze never leaving her face. How could his eyes be so black? Were they the deepest brown, or midnight blue like the waistcoat he'd worn the other night? And where had such a fanciful thought come from?

Remembering the true nature of his visit, she

pulled herself straight. "Yes. Lord and Lady Loburn were most insistent that I attend the interviews to protect the ladies' reputations and their sensibilities. I believe you also mentioned that my presence was required by your superior at the Ministry of Unnaturals?"

He scowled and his eyes narrowed, but after a long moment he seemed to realise this was one battle he wouldn't win. "Very well, if you are sure, but it will likely bore you."

"On the contrary, I have never found the pursuit of truth boring. I have spent the afternoon with Lady Loburn and Lady Elizabeth to narrow down the number of women whose privacy will be so rudely invaded." For how else could she describe the coming inquisition other than rude? Wycliff intended to demand whether blood pumped through their veins or not. A woman should never have to reveal the state of her heart to a strange man—and certainly not one who oozed such disapproval.

Had he been an equally rude child, or had adult-hood brought such a change about? Father had said it was the war and that Lord Wycliff's entire regi-ment had been slaughtered, but how had he survived? Hannah's curiosity, once aroused, was a monstrous beast to placate. It would demand to be fed information, but one look at Lord Wycliff dried up the questions upon her tongue. Perhaps she could nibble at him, like a little fish biting off small pieces that she could then put together to reveal the solved puzzle.

He removed his hat and tortured it for a moment in his hands. "That would be convenient. May I see the names?"

She removed the page from her pocket and held it for a moment before extending her arm. He took it with his fingertips, careful not to accidentally touch her. Hannah waited while he unfolded the sheet and scanned the neat script. "My father and I have hypothesised, given the known rate of infection among the *ton*, that there might have been between four and six Afflicted ladies present at the ball."

"That narrows the potential suspects, assuming we can identify them. What do your notations mean?" Dark brows drew together and he threw his question out without looking up from the list.

She laced her hands to still the nervous tremor—fielding his queries was like being asked algebra questions by a quarrelsome tutor. "Since they are deceased, legally the Afflicted cannot marry or inherit property. Nor, given their state, are they able to become *enceinte*. As such, we have noted those women who became engaged, married, inherited, or have borne children in the two years since the outbreak. We have also indicated those women who suffer any notable sickness that requires a beating heart."

He grunted. Was that approval...or a remnant of dinner lodged in his throat?

In the absence of any cues from him, Hannah continued, "There are a handful of ladies who are known to be Afflicted due to their advanced state of decay. Those unfortunates are identified."

"What of the others whom you know to be Afflicted but who conceal their state from society?" Now he did raise his gaze, drilling through her as he demanded that she betray her sex.

Wycliff asked too much. "I will not reveal what has been entrusted to me in confidence. Nor will I break the confidence of those who have sought a consultation with my father." There were some who moved in the highest circles, brushing shoulders with royalty, and none except those closest to them had any idea of their curse.

His fingers tightened on the list, curling the edges. "You would obstruct my investigation by withholding pertinent information?"

"While my father is at the forefront in researching the Afflicted curse, he is not the only physician in London. There may be many who have bought the silence of their doctors. I am not omnipotent, to know every such woman. I'm sure you consider yourself an astute man and you can deduce who is, and who is not, cursed among the remaining names." That was the most she could offer—her observations and knowledge learned at her father's side—but no one would be betrayed by loose words falling from her lips.

He stared at her and remained silent. Hannah was unused to conversation with gentlemen, especially when the scent of murder hung in the room. Should she offer him some tea while he appeared to think dark thoughts that brought storm clouds to hover over his head?

He ground his teeth and tucked the paper in a jacket pocket. "There would be no need for you to attend if you revealed the full extent of the information I require."

That riled. Quite apart from keeping secrets that were not hers to reveal, she had given an undertaking to Lord and Lady Loburn. "Your superior and Lady Loburn would disagree. I have promised that I will attend. That should suffice as a reason for my presence. As I have already stated, I have certain knowledge about the Unnatural affliction, gained at my father's side."

He made the noise deep in the back of his throat again. He really was quite rude. If Hannah could manage a conversation, surely he should be able to muster up something?

"Very well. We begin tomorrow morning. I cannot delay any longer. I will collect you at ten o'clock."

"I thought you might like to begin now. With

me." She placed her hands behind her back to stop the urge to fidget that sprang up under his scrutiny.

"You?" That gaze swept her form and catalogued all her faults.

"My name is on your list, for I attended last night. I am not married, nor have I ever known the joy of motherhood." *Nor will I*, the tiny voice reminded her. At twenty-two years of age, she was on the shelf. Her future consisted of caring for her parents, and then when the time came, taking up residence with Lizzie as her companion.

He made that noise again, a cross between a cough and a short bark. Perhaps he thought other people didn't deserve proper articulation of words and so he resorted to grunts, barks, and scoffing. "I will remove your name. I saw you in the ballroom and afterwards, when the body was discovered."

"Are you so easily convinced I am no Afflicted? No murderer?"

"You wore a pale yellow silk gown last evening. If you had cracked open the man's skull and devoured his brain in a frenzied attack, there would have been some trace of the crime upon your clothing. I saw none. To commit the crime, you would have needed a change of dress and an opportunity to wash. Nor do you show any signs of decay, and there is a flush to your cheeks that would indicate blood circulation. All of which leads me to conclude you are not one of the Afflicted."

Hannah swallowed. He had noticed the colour of her dress and the state of her cheeks? "Then we begin tomorrow morning, my lord."

He nodded and strode out without the scantest regard for civility.

Hannah sighed. "I suspect tomorrow will be a rather long day."

**7**

———

The next morning after breakfast, Hannah perched on the side of her mother's bed and stroked a silk rose embroidered on the coverlet. "Why did you ask Lady Loburn to add Viscount Wycliff to her guest list?"

Seraphina laughed and tapped her daughter's hand. "I should have anticipated you would discover that piece of information. How to explain what must now seem like an unforgivable imposition upon Lady Loburn?" She closed the book on her lap and placed it to one side. "The war against Napoleon is over, but the battle with his mages continues. One of them used foul dark arts to create this curse. He must be found and brought to justice for his heinous crime."

That Hannah could completely agree with. Those who used dark magic were frightening crea-tures who held themselves above the laws that

83

governed societies. If mages could act without sanction, there would be no limit to how they could twist the world with magic. "But how does Viscount Wycliff's presence at a ball aid in finding him?"

Seraphina waved her hands and a chessboard made of mist formed, to hover above the bed. Figures dropped onto the squares and at another wave of her hand, one advanced forward two places. "Magical battles are like games of chess. Pieces must be moved around the board in ways that sometimes don't have an obvious purpose. I don't know how the viscount will assist. I merely know he must be in play."

Hannah wondered which piece he would prove to be—a disposable pawn, or a noble knight? "I do not know how I shall make it through the next few days."

"You will endure because Lady Loburn has asked for your help and General Sir Manly Powers is relying on you to add a civilising touch to the proceedings. Not to mention the fact that you are more curious than ever about the brooding viscount." Seraphina wiped her arm across the ghostly board and it transformed into puffs of cloud that drifted away.

Was it curiosity? The man was a walking foul mood, as though only anger and bitterness flowed through his veins. Hannah would admit to mild curiosity about whether he could smile or laugh. The war had been horrid, but she wondered what about the campaign that resulted in the deaths of his men made him turn his back on society and unable to find any joy in life.

"I rather think spending time in his company will be similar to being stuck in a cave with an angry bear blocking the only exit. He might just bite off my head." Hannah would ensure the ladies on the list were offered a modicum of privacy and civility. Not just because the Ministry of Unnaturals requested it, but because it was what they deserved. But at what cost to herself?

Her mother picked up her hand and pressed it between her own. Beneath the cotton gloves her skin was cool. "If anyone knows how to handle a bear-headed man, it is you. You seem to manage your father when he's in one of his moods."

"I do not think you can liken the two men. Father's moods arise when he is tired but in the pursuit of knowledge. Lord Wycliff seems angry at the world in general."

A gentle huffing came from behind the veil as Seraphina laughed. "If anyone can ferret out the truth, it is you, my dear. But be careful. The discovery of secrets is often a reciprocal process."

"What do you mean?"

Her mother squeezed her hand. "To learn another's secret often means revealing one of your own."

Hannah didn't have many secrets and those she did hold would go with her to her grave. She wouldn't be surrendering them to Lord Wycliff, and so her curiosity about him might have to go unsatisfied. She decided to try a different tack. "Did you know Lord Wycliff during the war?"

"No. We mages were cloistered most of the time. I did little socialising outside of your father's friends, and when we ventured onto the battlefield, we were heavily guarded." A wistful tone touched her mother's voice.

Did Mother likewise suffer in her loneliness? Being born a mage had limited her social circle. She had held a high rank while alive, but many people were frightened by the concept of a female mage, as though she were the extremis of an Unnatural creature. But then a true love match had saved her mother from the ache of an empty heart. There was no such knight on the horizon for Hannah.

"But you will always have Father," Hannah whispered.

"Oh, Hannah. If I could only summon sufficient power, I would turn back the hands of time and give you the introduction to society you deserve and the chance to find your own true love." Her mother claimed no ability to read minds, but she often knew Hannah's innermost thoughts. A gloved hand reached out and wiped away a single tear that escaped the corner of Hannah's eye.

"I have so much, it is selfish of me to want more." Hannah mustered a smile and willed herself to stop dwelling on what her life lacked, and to count her blessings instead. She had two parents who loved and indulged her. She had a roof over her head, clothes on her back, and books to expand her mind. What more could a young lady desire?

*Companionship and a passionate love.*

"I think you need a dog," her mother announced.

"A dog?" Hannah blinked, wondering what detour in the conversation she had missed.

"Yes. Leave it to me. Now, you had better trot downstairs and wait in the parlour. I suspect the viscount will expect you to run out the door the moment his carriage stops outside the house." Lady Miles rested her hands over the pages of her book.

"I shall tell you all that transpires upon my return." Hannah kissed the muslin covering her mother's face. "A dog?" she muttered as she left her mother's room and headed down to the parlour.

Hannah didn't have sufficient time to sit idle. She shrugged on a grey pelisse trimmed in navy that matched her dress. Next, a straw bonnet with navy ribbons tied under her chin. Then, just as the old grandfather clock in the hall began to strike ten, the carriage pulled up outside. Like a character in a fairy tale, she wondered if she needed to make it to the end of the path before the last chime sounded. Although if she were turned into a pumpkin, she hoped her mother could reverse such a spell.

With a tight grip on her reticule, she headed out the front door. On closer inspection, the carriage appeared rather shabby and covered in dust, and was devoid of any crest. A man in plain clothing hopped down from the box and held the door open for her.

The horses weren't quite a matched pair, one being a dark bay and the other a brown. They passed the casual glance, but a second look highlighted the difference in their colour.

*A hired conveyance*, Hannah thought as she stepped inside.

The viscount didn't even bother to get out and greet her. But then, he wasn't courting her, only collecting an employee. Hannah cast herself in the role of secretary to the viscount's inquisitor. Today his usual black was relieved by a waistcoat of a green so deep it was like the hidden depths of a dense forest.

"Good morning, Lord Wycliff," Hannah said as she took the seat beside him but kept to the far edge. The viscount might lack basic civilities, but she would keep a courteous tongue.

"Miss Miles. At least you are prompt, unlike other members of your sex." He nodded his head and rapped his cane on the carriage roof. "We shall visit the late Lady Albright first."

An obvious target. Lady Albright had been one of only two veiled women in attendance at Lizzie's party, and hers was a sad tale.

The passing of the Unnaturals Act in 1812 gave all Unnaturals the same rights as ordinary Englishmen. They were also subject to the same laws. Since the Afflicted had no pulse but refused to go quietly into their graves, Parliament had declared them to be dead and a type of Unnatural creature.

English law stated that the dead could not marry, inherit, or hold property. Set aside by her husband, the late Lady Albright now eked out an existence relying on the charity of friends and family. She and Lady Loburn were close friends and Lizzie considered her an aunt, hence her inclusion at the celebration.

"You think the late Lady Albright might have committed such a heinous murder?" Hannah couldn't fit the description of murderer to the older woman, who retained a quiet dignity despite the cruel treatment meted out by her husband's hand. She was rather fond of knitting and Hannah tried to imagine her brandishing knitting needles as fatal weapons. No, never on an innocent man. Although no one would be surprised if her husband were found with a knitting needle thrust into his jugular one day.

Wycliff's gaze swept over Hannah and carried on to fix on something in the landscape outside. "A veil or mask could hide so much and I do not know what the Afflicted are capable of. They have already proven themselves able to commit such a crime."

"A veil doesn't conceal the true nature of a person, only the state of their exterior. Lady Albright has always been a kind and gentle woman. She has honour in her soul, unlike her husband." Hannah bit her lip to stop herself from saying more. The viscount created an unusual reaction in her and she felt herself on the verge of an argument.

Wycliff grunted, but refused to turn his attention to the inside of the carriage. Hannah was used to being ignored, so she occupied herself by mentally reviewing the previous day's autopsy results. Why had the unfortunate woman's heart rotted? Sir Hugh had unlocked his safe, where he kept a portion of the face powder, to infect a new trio of mice. They would observe the creatures as the disease took hold and stilled their hearts, looking for signs that the passage of time affected the curse and likewise changed the effect on its victims.

Hannah was so engrossed in her internal obser-vations that she failed to notice the carriage coming to a stop. A cough that sounded distinctly like a grumble came from beside her and she looked around and blinked, taking a moment to orient herself.

Wycliff arched a dark brow. "When you are ready. Although I suppose I should be thankful you didn't feel the need to fill the silence with vacuous chatter."

Hannah opened her mouth to comment, then snapped it shut again. The man was insufferable, but she refused to give him the satisfaction of seeing her rise to his bait. Instead, she clutched her reticule in one hand and placed the other on the side of the carriage as she stepped to the ground. Unassisted.

They were in a middle-class neighbourhood with a tidy row of modest brick town houses. Hannah had a vague recollection that the late Lady Albright now lived with a cousin.

Wycliff charged past her up the front path and rapped sharply with the cast-iron knocker. Hannah trailed behind and wondered whether the man would temper his blunt edges when dealing with the tragic resident.

A maid in a white cap answered the door, glanced at Wycliff, and then visibly retreated back into the house. Hannah let out a sigh. She should carry a bucket of water to extinguish the numerous fires the viscount would no doubt ignite.

Inside the cool interior, Hannah followed the tails of Wycliff's coat, which flicked at a corner and disappeared into a side room. Voices came from beyond. By the time Hannah reached the door, two startled women were rising from their seats and the maid was hiding in a corner behind the tea table.

The late Lady Albright wore dark grey with her customary heavy black veil pinned to her cap. The veil dropped over her shoulders and came well below the high neck of her dress. Like Hannah's mother, gloves covered her hands and were tucked under the long sleeves of her gown. The other woman wore a bright orange morning dress and looked to be in her mid-fifties. Both women stared at Wycliff as though a hound from Hell had just charged into their parlour.

"Lady Albright," Hannah said and bobbed a curtsey, ignoring the viscount. "I do not believe I have had the pleasure of meeting your cousin?"

The veiled woman took a step closer and gestured to the Gerbera daisy at her side. "Miss Miles, may I introduce my cousin, Mrs Hamilton?"

Heads were nodded, and knees dipped.

"I'm sure you know Viscount Wycliff," Hannah murmured.

On hearing his name, the man finally offered a scant bow. "I am here to discuss the murder that occurred at the Marquess of Loburn's ball. I desire to know your whereabouts during the evening."

Lady Albright put a hand to her chest and the veil fluttered closer to her face with her indrawn gasp. "Surely you do not suspect me?"

"I suspect all the Afflicted in attendance that night, until I have eliminated them as being responsible." He clasped his hands behind his back, the move of a soldier making himself comfortable.

Hannah approached the older woman, offered an apologetic smile to her cousin, and then took Lady Albright's gloved hands in hers. She drew the woman toward a chaise and urged her to sit.

"If I am not required for this interview, I have duties to attend to." Mrs Hamilton gestured for the maid to follow her and departed.

"Take your time to answer," Hannah said. She ignored the glare heating the middle of her back. The man could learn to wait. The footman was dead, and giving the Afflicted woman a chance to gather her thoughts wouldn't bring him back.

"Did you see that Lord Albright was in attendance with the new Lady Albright? She recently gave him a second son and he is much enamoured of her." The light tone of the late Lady Albright's words was unable to mask the deeper heartache beneath.

Hannah had heard the twitter among the other women. They had hoped for a spectacle when the deceased wife met the living one. They were sadly disappointed when the late Lady Albright had not an unkind word to say about her replacement.

"Yes. I heard. It must be very difficult for you." The Afflicted suffered in more ways than the original curse. Lady Miles had been rejected by society for her magical abilities; dying and being numbered among the Afflicted made little difference to her. Others felt the loss of their status and friends more keenly.

Wycliff tapped a toe. "Your movements, Lady Albright."

She raised her head, only the barest facial details visible through the thick veil. "I do not dance, and therefore I was happy to chaperone the younger people while they chatted. I spent most of the evening to one side, by the entrance to the dining room. Numerous people saw me there. I am some-what distinctive," she said, one hand resting briefly on her veil. She then gave the names of several young courting couples she had supervised that night. Wycliff jotted the names in a small notebook.

"Did you see the butterflies that Mother creat-ed?" Hannah had looked for the older woman in the crowd but failed to find her.

"I left early and am sorry I missed the wonderful enchantment. I found I had no stamina for staying overlong." The black veil bobbed with each syllable.

*Poor thing*, Hannah thought. It would be taxing to gaze upon a cruel husband and his beautiful wife while others waited for your façade to crack.

Wycliff fixed Lady Albright with a hard stare. "When did you last feed?"

Hannah was glad that his behaviour meant no one had rung for tea, or she might have choked on her drink.

Lady Albright rose on unsteady legs and her gloved hands went to her neck. She pulled forth a long silver chain with a small key at the end. She crossed the parlour and fitted the key into a cabinet that rested on the sideboard. She opened the door to reveal the contents.

Inside sat a jar, much like those used to preserve fruit. Slivers of what appeared to be some pale vegetable floated in a clear liquid.

"My husband may have cast me aside, but my

friends have not. Lady Loburn ensures I have a monthly delivery. I am no starving monster, if that is what you seek."

"Can anyone verify what time you left the ball?" Wycliff asked.

Lady Albright gestured to the open doorway. "You can ask my cousin's maid. She opened the door to admit me when I returned."

Wycliff grunted and made another note in the little book, after which he replaced it in a jacket pocket. "Come, Miss Miles, we have much to do."

With that, he strode from the room.

Lady Albright shook her head as she closed and locked the cabinet. "I do not envy you, Miss Miles, if they expect you to keep him in check."

"He is somewhat of a bolting horse." Hannah sat for a moment, since her mind baulked at following him like an obedient puppy.

"Better hope he does not break a leg on uneven ground," Lady Albright said.

Hannah rose and dipped her knees, the angle of her head concealing the slight smile that touched her lips. From her brief acquaintance with the viscount, he did have a tendency to rush in without checking the lay of the land first. Was that why Lady Loburn had insisted she attend the interviews with the viscount—in case he hurled one insult too many?

Hannah found the pavement devoid of the viscount, but the carriage door hung open. As she steeled herself for close quarters, she spied a familiar face—the young woman who had wept over her spoilt gown at the Loburn ball. The two of them glanced at each other and the woman stopped with a shy smile as recognition bloomed between them.

Bother. They had not been formally introduced and as such, they weren't supposed to talk to one another. But they had already broken that rule over a ruined dress.

Hannah dropped a quick curtsey. "I am Miss Hannah Miles."

Her new acquaintance mimicked her action. "Miss Emma Knightley."

*Oh dear.* Hannah knew that name—it was on Lord Wycliff's list. She hadn't been able to conjure a face to go with the name when she had discussed the woman with Lizzie and Lady Loburn. Of the same age as Hannah, Miss Knightley's fiancé had called off their engagement two years ago and she had not made any new connections.

Hannah glanced to the carriage. She could alert Lord Wycliff, but the footpath with so many people around was no place for a woman to be harangued by the man about her unnatural appetites. The woman deserved the privacy of her own parlour.

"Did you manage to remove the stain from your dress?" Hannah asked.

Emma glanced down at her gown, a sensible striped cotton much like the one Hannah wore. It appeared neither of them had the disposable income to stay abreast of fashion. "No, sadly. But I believe I shall be able to cover the mark with some embroidery."

"Salvageable then, at least." Hannah kept the smile on her face as she inspected her counterpart. The rise and fall of Miss Knightley's chest was irregular and shallow, as though it were no instinct, but a deliberate exercise she had to remember. In the morning light, there was a slight grey pallor to her face under the layer of powder. The faint whiff of cloves confirmed it.

"Yes. If you'll excuse me, I must be on my way. My parents are expecting me."

They bobbed their goodbyes and Hannah watched the other woman thread her way through the pedestrians.

"Oh, dear. Another one," she whispered.

Miss Knightley was one of the Afflicted and Hannah didn't think the stain on her dress had been red wine. Perhaps Lord Wycliff would finally muster up a smile when she told him the news, right before he admonished her for not dragging him from the carriage to interrogate the poor woman.

**8**

---

By the time Hannah stepped into the carriage, Lord Wycliff was staring intently at his pocket watch. Silent disapproval at Hannah's failure to rush after him imbued the very air in the shabby interior. He huffed as he snapped the timepiece shut and dropped it back into his waist-coat pocket.

You would almost think he was late for an appointment with the Prince Regent, the way he glared from Hannah to the neighbourhood in general. No doubt he suspected them of conspiring to disrupt his orderly plans.

The viscount rapped on the carriage roof. Then he pulled out the list and crossed off the name of Lady Albright.

"I met Miss Emma Knightley just now," Hannah

told him. "You can change her notation—she is indeed one of the Afflicted. Last evening I saw her in the front parlour, with a most unusual stain on her dress that she said was red wine." Hannah rushed through a confession that felt like a monumental betrayal of the other woman. Now she had set the viscount on Miss Knightley's trail.

Lord Wycliff's eyebrows shot up. Would he smile...? No. Not quite, but for once he didn't look entirely displeased. He ran a finger down the list and then scribbled something next to her name. "Why didn't you call me?"

"I hardly think the footpath was the appropriate place to air Miss Knightley's private business." The man really did lack the most basic regard for common decency.

He huffed and put his list away. "We will call on her after the others, once she has had time to reach home."

Two more women were visited, questioned, and found to be entirely ordinary. Their names were likewise struck through with a heavy hand. One admitted behind her fan to Hannah that she was in a *delicate condition*, but the news was not yet public. As soon as he caught the whispered words with what seemed to be bat-like hearing, Viscount Wycliff swept out of her parlour without so much as a nod goodbye.

Another woman choked on her biscuit at the mere suggestion she might be one of the Afflicted and had to be thumped on the back by her footman. Wycliff grunted, called Hannah to heel, and left the premises. Apparently nearly choking to death was sufficient to be removed from his list of suspects.

Next they tried the modest Knightley family home, only to be told that Miss Knightley was out. How odd. She had told Hannah she was returning home directly.

"I shall return tomorrow," the viscount said, and barely waited for Hannah to take her seat before instructing the carriage to move on. As the carriage rumbled through the streets to the next address, his dark regard turned to her. "This process would be accelerated if you would reveal the Afflicted on the list."

"As I have already told you, Lord Wycliff, I am not omnipotent. There are thousands of peers in London and only two to three hundred Afflicted, and I am not acquainted with every single one. I know some and can guess at others, but many have not revealed themselves and are entitled to keep their state private." The more he snapped, the more Hannah fought to block his barbs.

Being in the man's presence was exhausting. Hannah thought he might accidentally smile or laugh over the course of the day, but not a single shaft of sunlight broke through his thundercloud demeanour. How she wished her mother's mage blood coursed through her veins, so that she could call down an actual lightning bolt to strike him! That would give him something to pout about.

The mismatched horses pulled them toward Mayfair and another ambush-style interview. Hannah stared out the window as Londoners went about their daily lives. How many Unnaturals were concealed among the hustle and bustle of activity? Did commoners rub shoulders with vampyres, lycanthropes, or selkies as they went about their day?

The Afflicted like her mother were just one type of creature that defied Nature's laws. There were many more that the government sought to number and administer under the new Ministry. Even the army had a regiment composed of vicious lycanthropes who terrorised the enemy with gnashing teeth. Or did they only do that in newspaper illustrations? Hannah had not met a lycanthrope in person, so could not judge how many teeth they showed.

"What do you know of Lady Gabriella Ridlington?" the viscount asked, pulling her attention back inside the carriage.

Hannah knew of the earl's daughter by name and reputation only, neither of which painted her in a favourable light. They rarely crossed paths and when they did, such as on the night of the ball, there was usually some subtle put-down at Hannah's expense. The lady had declared she would never marry, which raised Hannah's suspicions as to the state of her heart. If she possessed one.

"I believe she is an Afflicted, but we do not move in the same circles, so I cannot confirm my suspicion. She has never journeyed to consult with my father, although he is not the only scientist working to find a way to reverse their condition."

The earl kept a large house in London, set well back from the road and guarded by wrought iron gates. The dusty hired carriage stopped outside the grand home. Lord Wycliff opened the door and jumped down before the footman could bustle over.

For once, he actually turned and offered a hand to Hannah. She blinked at him, then laid her hand in his as she stepped down. His skin seemed warmer than normal under her glove and he snatched it away as though *she* had burned *him*.

"I wish to speak to Lady Gabriella Ridlington," Wycliff said to the butler.

Hannah hung back. The grandeur of the house and the haughty demeanour of its occupant loomed over her and pressed her to the tiles of the foyer. How she longed to disappear into the panelling, but the entrance was bright and white and there were no dark corners to hide her. There wasn't even a palm large enough to conceal her, only alabaster busts on narrow plinths that were eerily similar in appearance to Hannah's fabric-draped mother.

"Lady Gabriella is not at home to callers today, my lord," the man replied.

Wycliff fixed him with a withering stare. "She will see me. I am on official business for the Ministry of Unnaturals, investigating a murder. I can always return with a troop of soldiers to seize her and take her away for questioning, if she would prefer."

The man blanched and hurried away. He returned mere moments later and gestured for them to follow him. A short distance down a wide hallway, he pushed open double doors and bowed. "Lord Wycliff, my lady, and another."

*And another.* Hannah didn't even warrant a name or a scant description. Perhaps she did a better job of blending in with the walls than she thought.

The man stepped back to allow them to enter. The lady in question reclined on a chaise in an opulent parlour. Waterfall silk in a pale blue adorned the walls. The sofas were upholstered in cream and blue. Dark blue drapes hung from a soaring ceiling and dropped to the floor with the drama of stage curtains.

Lady Gabriella was clad in sunburst yellow, the only bold punch of colour among the hues of blue and cream. She shone like a star in the sky. In one hand she held a fan of ostrich feathers, the plumes dyed a deep navy, and fanned herself with leisurely strokes. "This is the most horrid intrusion. I do hope no one saw you arrive."

Wycliff strode to the middle of the room, while Hannah edged around the sides and stopped to admire a selection of Wedgwood plates that complemented the room's colour scheme.

"I am an agent of the Ministry of Unnaturals, tasked with investigating a heinous murder." Wycliff flicked out his coattails and took a seat on the opposite chaise, without waiting to be asked to sit. "I wish to know of your movements during the evening of the Loburn ball."

Hannah remained standing and hoped that if she kept still, no one would notice she was there.

Lady Gabriella rose to a sitting position and leaned her elbow on the rolled end of the chaise.

Hannah moved closer to contemplate the other woman's cool beauty. The aristocrat possessed skin so delicate one could almost see the blue veins running beneath. Her eyes were the crisp blue of a clear summer's day. Blonde hair was arranged in a cascade of curls that brushed against her cheeks.

Another woman blessed by Nature with the ideal English peaches-and-cream beauty. Hannah thought of the noblewoman like the finest milled white bread served to royalty, whereas she was the rougher and darker grained loaf consumed by the common folk.

"As ever, I was surrounded by a number of most attentive beaux. Do you require all their names?" Lady Gabriella asked.

One beau in particular, from what Hannah had observed of their tête-à-tête outside the ballroom. "There was a gentleman who was most solicitous of you last evening, but I could not place him."

A cold stare glanced to Hannah and then back to Wycliff. "Mr Jonathon Rowley. He is not titled, but he possesses sufficient income for me to overlook his lack of noble birth. He is indeed most enamoured of me. His family own a number of smelly breweries, but they have branched out into a more suitable line of business. They import champagne and have quite a select clientele."

There was something in Lady Gabriella's expression that nagged at Hannah. Something not quite right. Or perhaps it was the opposite—she was too perfect, like a finely crafted doll. Not a single blemish or spot marred her appearance. Even her eyebrows were perfection and probably took a maid a full hour with a tiny brush to sculpt their dramatic arches.

Hannah lowered her eyes but stared at the other young woman, trying to discern what clues her subconscious had noticed. Yes, there. The artful curls about her face concealed the faint edge of a mask at her hairline.

The fan aided the illusion, as the slow movement of the navy feathers meant it was harder to focus on the smaller details of her face that would reveal the mask. While Lady Gabriella's eyebrows were a masterpiece, with each hair embedded in the porcelain, they were incapable of expressing any subtle emotion.

The finest masks were crafted by those with magic coursing through their veins. They created ceramics that could mimic the muscle movement underneath the cool surface. But that movement didn't quite seem right when you concentrated on it. They were stiff, like the material of which the mask was made, and not the fluid movement of skin.

With the other woman's status confirmed, Hannah pondered how to alert Lord Wycliff to the clues. Lunging forward and ripping off the delicate mask while proclaiming *Aha!* seemed uncalled for, no matter how satisfying she might find it. She turned her head and tried to attract the viscount's attention. Not an easy thing to do, since he seemed intent on ignoring Hannah's presence, all his focus on Lady Gabriella.

Hannah coughed as though something had lodged in her throat, which earned her a scowl from both parties.

"Do you require a glass of water?" Wycliff asked with drawn brows.

"No, thank you." Between coughs, when he deigned to look at her, Hannah mouthed the word *mask* and tapped the side of her face. She hoped the viscount caught her direction and that it went over the head of Gabriella, who appeared to be contemplating her fingernails.

Wycliff arched one black eyebrow, then directed his intense stare at the noblewoman. After a long pause he said, "Your mask is quite exquisite. The porcelain is almost sheer and allows your mouth some movement. Is it Venetian?"

The ostrich feathers stilled. Lady Gabriella raised one hand and almost touched her cheek. "Yes. They have magically gifted artisans who are masters of porcelain masks. Most men cannot tell, even upon the closest inspection. A man can kiss my lips and never notice."

The fan dropped and Hannah found herself compelled to stare at the lush pink lips. She held her tongue, so she didn't reveal her lack of information about kissing. Did lips not stray when kissing, so that a man wouldn't notice the thin edge of the mask? Putting aside whatever lips did, how did a man take a woman in his arms and fail to notice the absence of a beating heart in her chest?

She tucked the question away to ask her mother that evening. Or Lizzie might know, now that she had tasted of her lovely duke.

One black eyebrow arched and the viscount's lip on the same side was pulled upward as though the two were connected by a string. "Not all men are so easily fooled, I assure you."

Hannah bit her lip to hold in a snort. He *had* been fooled until she had alerted him to the mask. However, if the viscount was throwing barbs at another, it gave her a rest. Not that any person, deceased or not, deserved to bear the brunt of his foul mood.

"Perhaps you haven't kissed the right woman, my lord, that you fail to be swept away in the moment." The fan began its dance up and down once more.

He withdrew a notebook from his pocket and a slim silver pencil. "Did you dance with anyone that evening?"

Gabriella laughed and turned her perfect face to the viscount. "I assure you, Lord Wycliff, my dance card was full. Mr Rowley quite monopolised my time and I barely had the opportunity to dance with half a dozen other eligible men."

Hannah had managed one dance—with her father. She wished the floor would open up and swallow her. She was as empty as the hollowed-out woman on her father's autopsy table. How marvellous it must be, to know yourself to be beautiful and desired. To have men swarming around you like bees on sugar syrup. Why did some women have all the attention while others had none?

Hannah's needs were simple: one man who adored her would more than suffice for a lifetime.

"I will require your dance card." Wycliff stared at Gabriella, his brows pulled together like angry caterpillars about to do battle with one another.

Lady Gabriella folded the fan and pointed it at

Hannah. "Miss Miles, do make yourself useful and pull the bell."

Hannah drew a deep breath to stop herself from bobbing a curtsey. Lady Gabriella might treat her as a servant, but that didn't mean she had to act like one. With quiet, measured steps she walked to the tasselled pull by the door. She gave it one short tug.

The conversation continued without her.

"It is curious that your card was full when, given your state, you can never marry or present a man with the necessary heir," Lord Wycliff said.

Lady Gabriella's face remained impassive, a permanent half smile caught in the porcelain. Only her eyes revealed her changes of mood. The blue froze over, like water that has turned to ice. "Certainly, when I announced that I would never marry, it was a most severe blow to the eligible men of the *ton*. Then a curious thing occurred. I find being dead brings with it a certain...freedom. Men are odd creatures. When you remove the obligations of marriage and offspring, they have flocked to enjoy my company in increasing numbers."

Wycliff made that little grunt in the back of his throat. Hannah decided it was a noise of slight incredulity, as though he thought the speaker wasn't being entirely truthful.

The butler who had admitted them slipped back into the room and awaited further instructions.

The ostrich feathers glided through the air. "Ask

Breton to fetch my dance card from the Loburn ball. Wycliff wishes to number my admirers."

"My lady." The butler bowed and disappeared as silently as he had come.

"Did you leave the ballroom at any time?" The silver pencil was poised over the notebook.

"I do not want for a thing, Lord Wycliff. My father is wealthy and influential in the House of Lords. I have benefactors who are close to the Prince Regent. I assure you, I am protected and cosseted like a valuable jewel. If you are looking for a starving Afflicted who would stoop to feeding on a footman, then I suggest you try the lesser nobles who are without my resources to feed their hunger."

If this were a tennis match, then Hannah wasn't quite sure which party had scored the match point. Lady Gabriella did have a most convincing argument. Why would she fall upon the footman in a sudden murderous hunger? From the way Mr Rowley had stared at her, Lady Gabriella was in more danger of being devoured by him.

"How does your mother manage, Miss Miles? I imagine it was quite a tumble for your family, stripped of your mother's privileges when her pulse stopped. However do you make ends meet? Or do you scrimp on fashion to ensure she is fed?" Lady Gabriella laughed, a tinkling sound with a harsh edge.

Hannah dug her nails into her palms to stop a

heated retort. She would not rise to the bait. Women like Lady Gabriella thrived on the visible suffering of others. Hannah's gown was a few seasons old. The cut was functional, the fabric robust, the stripe and colour plain. She saw no need for the latest fashions only to cover them with her canvas apron while she handled another woman's internal organs.

Although now she had a hankering to crack open Lady Gabriella's chest to examine the state of her heart and determine if it were as rotten as her character.

"Our needs are few and we manage quite well. Thank you for your concern." With some effort, Hannah managed to keep a pleasant smile on her face, her tone neutral.

The other woman narrowed her eyes. "Well, perhaps it's a blessing you are not out in society. Your sort can probably muddle through with only one or two old gowns. Whereas I must suffer through weekly appointments with my modiste to keep up my appearance."

"Yes, I am quite blessed that I am not in your situation," Hannah agreed.

Further salvos were silenced by the butler returning with the requested dance card. He handed it to the viscount, who scanned the lines of names.

For the first time in their brief acquaintance, Hannah was glad of the viscount's abrupt nature. He tucked the dance card in a pocket along with his notebook and pencil, and stood. This time he inclined his head to Lady Gabriella. "I have no further questions."

Then he strode from the room and Hannah gladly followed in his wake.

# 9

The next morning, bad weather threatened and Hannah's mother declared her intention to sit out in the garden. Or *the damnable Amazonian wilds*, as her father called it. Hannah trailed a hand over foliage as she followed her father through the trees, her mother in his arms.

Seraphina had a particular affinity for nature and in their time at the house, she had encouraged trees to soar on the bare plot. Now the house looked as though it had been built in the depths of a forest hundreds of years ago. Branches laced overhead to filter out the sunlight. Ferns and flowering ground cover scrambled among trunks and roots. Hannah had loved to explore the undergrowth as a child, and spent many a happy hour pretending she was an explorer lost in a strange world. Now she saw the large trees as offering sanctuary from all that happened in London.

Lady Gabriella was welcome to her lush parlour. In spring, Hannah preferred to be surrounded by delicate, lace-like ferns.

By the stream that ran down one side of the property was a sweep of lawn that brushed the sides of the water. A wooden bower, its back to the trees, was covered in damask roses, magically encouraged to bloom almost continuously and their greenery sheltered a cushioned bench. On the other bank of the stream, a laurel hedge almost looked civilised as it bounded the side they shared with a neighbour.

Her father fussed and arranged the cushions behind her mother. "It is going to rain. Sera, are you sure this is wise?"

"You know I adore the rain. Now, off to your laboratory with you, Hugh. Hannah and I need some womanly time alone." She pushed him away with a laugh.

"Enough said. I'll leave you to it." He kissed his wife's cheek through the veil and then saluted before disappearing through the trees.

Hannah sat on a blanket at her mother's feet. Overhead, she watched clouds gather and crash into one another. Judging by the darkening grey above, her mother would not have to wait long for the rain. Hannah tried to find shapes and objects in the clouds, but there were too many devouring each other and she could only conjure Viscount Wycliff's frown.

The laurel hedge rustled and shook and attracted Hannah's curiosity. When she turned her head, the row of clipped branches undulated as though a sea monster skimmed beneath the greenery. Branches sprouted up and sideways until they reformed into a unicorn. Opposite, a dragon grew from the greenery and flapped its twiggy wings. The unicorn bowed its head and used its horn to parry the dragon.

Hannah watched the two shrubbery actors, but the swirling storm above called her more. She heaved a sigh as a particularly dark cloud enveloped its neighbours.

Seraphina lowered her hands and the unicorn and dragon sank back into the hedge. "You used to find great amusement in my cavorting topiary."

Hannah tipped back her head to bestow an upside-down smile on her mother. "I'm sorry, Mother. I find I have too much on my mind."

Her mother picked a dusky yellow rose and twirled it between her fingers. "Such as a gruesome murder?"

"Yes. The circumstances bother me and are a constant niggle in my mind." Hannah lived with death and helped her father put it under a microscope in his laboratory, but this particular instance haunted her waking moments.

"Well, it certainly put a dampener on Lizzie's

grand engagement ball. It took some work to ensure it didn't reach the newspapers." Seraphina tucked the rose behind a veiled ear.

Hannah watched one dark grey cloud crash into another and swallow it to produce a larger and angrier-looking cloud. "That timing indeed bothers me. Who would do such a thing to Lizzie? But it is more—" How to give voice to the growing unease within her?

"Pick a point at which to begin unravelling your thoughts, dearest." Her mother's voice was soothing, like the babble of the river.

It was indeed a slight to Lizzie, to mar her engagement ball in such a fashion, but had that been the primary goal of the murderer or an unintended consequence?

"Why commit such a crime at a ball with two hundred people in attendance? The risk of discovery was high. Revellers were roaming the house, as were the staff." How was it no one had seen anything? Or perhaps the activity was the perfect mask; with so many people bustling around the house it was impossible to pinpoint who, if any, had done something criminal.

"Perhaps it was a crime of great impulse. A moment glimpsed and seized." Seraphina stroked a hand through the air and the laurel hedge trimmed itself with a neat line along the top.

"That is Viscount Wycliff's theory. That one of

the Afflicted committed the murder while in the grips of a great hunger. Unfortunately, we did see two such murders when the curse first struck. Yet, we know that an Afflicted in such an extreme state would be agitated and incoherent. What some would call raving mad. This murderer moved undetected among those present and committed their crime in a place where they found one person alone. While it might have been opportunistic, it shows some presence of mind. A starving Afflicted would have leapt upon someone in the ballroom."

*That* was what worried at Hannah. The explanation seemed plausible, yet it didn't fit with the behaviour of those at the ball. Were they missing something and an Afflicted had become capable of such a heinous crime for some other reason than an overriding hunger? Was this little more than an old-fashioned murder performed by an Afflicted...lashing out when something was spilled on her dress or in frustration at the cruel actions of a former husband?

"An interesting observation, Miss Miles."

Hannah sat up to find the dark cloud had dropped from the sky to ruin her enjoyment of the garden.

"Lord Wycliff," Seraphina said.

He inclined his head, apparently locating his manners in the presence of a mage. "Forgive me, the maid said you were in the garden and I offered to find my own way." He placed his hands in the small of his back, an action often done unconsciously by men who had spent a lifetime in the military.

Hannah realised her hair had pulled free of its knot and she gathered up the loose strands, searching to find the pins to secure them. "Shall I fetch Papa to carry you in, Mother?"

Her mother waved a gloved hand. "No, thank you, dear. You know how much I enjoy it when nature puts on a tempestuous display. I shall stay here awhile longer."

*A FEW MINUTES EARLIER...*

WYCLIFF GLARED at the maid and said he would find Miss Miles himself. How difficult would it be to walk through to the garden? As it turned out, it was no garden, but an untamed forest. Trees crowded the space and obscured the open paddocks beyond. The forest could have hidden a multitude of the enemy waiting to ambush the unwary. He trod with light feet on the winding path and wished he had a sword in his hand.

A rustling made him stop, his senses alert to danger. A peacock appeared from under a bush and crossed his path, dragging its train. One feather snagged on the undergrowth and the unblinking luminous eye stared at him. He shouldn't be surprised to see the bird here. Peacocks were much favoured by mages in the casting of their spells. Sir Manly had commissioned a crest for the Ministry of Unnaturals that would feature the all-seeing eye.

He continued on and the path opened out by the river with a narrow ribbon of lawn. The younger woman, the one with a pulse, lay on the grass staring at the clouds. Her mother sat in a bower and resembled a marble bust draped in linen that had been left on a bench, instead of placed atop a plinth.

He paused before he burst out of the undergrowth, as Miss Miles's voice drifted through the ferns and shrubs.

"—a starving Afflicted would have leapt upon someone in the ballroom."

As an investigator for the Ministry of Unnaturals, he was privy to confidential information about the undead women, such as their indelicate and inhumane appetite for human brains. His files contained notes about how such creatures acted when hungry, but he had not considered it relevant to his investigation. He had thought the nature of their craving sufficient. Now Miss Miles's comment made him consider events in a new light.

"An interesting observation, Miss Miles," he said as he stepped into the thick grass.

"Lord Wycliff," Lady Miles said.

He inclined his head to what had once been the

most revered mage in England. Being in the presence of what was left of the woman made his hackles rise. It was unnerving to be unable to see her face. The hairs on his body lifted in response to being near her, just as when he stepped outside in the depths of winter without a thick overcoat.

Miss Miles sat up, her long, dark hair pulling free of a careless knot at the crown of her head. Strands brushed her skin and his hand itched to discover if they were as smooth as the silk they resembled. A foolish notion. He was simply overtired from conducting his enquiries all night and for most of the morning.

"Shall I fetch Papa to carry you in, Mother?"

Lady Miles waved a gloved hand. "No, thank you, dear. You know how much I enjoy it when nature puts on a tempestuous display. I shall stay here awhile longer."

Miss Miles glanced at him, then away, as she gathered up her hair and pushed pins through loose locks. "Are you so sure it was one of the Afflicted and not some person with a personal motive against the unfortunate footman?"

He bit back his initial retort. Or course he had investigated the personal life of the unremarkable footman, one Roger Dunn—that was what had occupied him for the last several hours. As it transpired, the dead man's life made a particularly boring book to read. "Personal grudges usually result in a quick knife to the back in a darkened alley. Scooping out Dunn's brains seems rather unnecessary if he had gambling debts or had dallied with another man's wife."

"A starving Afflicted wouldn't have had the presence of mind to lie in wait in a secluded area of the house." For a moment, those coffee-coloured eyes rested on him and a flare of rebellion made them come alive.

He stared at her, trying to uncover some fault to dampen his growing fascination, until she looked away and broke his fixed gaze. "I wish to conduct more interviews this afternoon. We are nearly through the list and once we are, we can be done with one another. I particularly want to find Miss Emma Knightley."

Miss Miles rose and brushed out her skirts. "Of course. I shall fetch my bonnet and shawl."

Wycliff took a step to the side to allow her to pass and her form was soon swallowed by the forest. That left him alone with the undead mage. Social conversation was never his strong suit, so he watched the ripples of water passing over the rocks instead.

"I think Hannah needs a dog for company. What do you think, Lord Wycliff? I hear dogs offer unswerving loyalty."

"If you deserve such devotion, then yes, canines are loyal until death." He didn't like the topic of conversation and instead kept his attention on the stream. Were there any fish? Then a rock wriggled and jumped, as though it were a fish trying to make its way upstream.

*Mage trickery*. He snorted.

"There are those who believe I lost my powers when my pulse stopped."

He had never spared much thought for the ways of mages, apart from wishing they acted faster in the heat of battle. Nor were they ever around when you truly needed them, when your men were being slaughtered in the dark by otherworldly assailants. "England has always had twelve mages. When one dies, their power is transferred to another. On your death, a boy was born, in Norfolk I believe, with your mage powers."

The rock kept leaping upstream, playing leapfrog with the other rocks until it came to settle in a wide, flat area.

"England now has thirteen mages," she said pleasantly. "An unprecedented situation."

He stared at the rock, waiting to see what it would do next. Why were they having this conversation? Events had drawn him into working for the Ministry of Unnaturals. That didn't mean he wanted to be intimately acquainted with such creatures. "England only has twelve who possess a pulse."

Birdsong came from above. A single high note trilled and then fell silent.

"Quite. I found on my death that my power had made a similar transition."

That made him turn and his own pulse raced faster. Did a dead mage wield powers given by death? Was it possible she knew something of Hell and how to escape its clutches? "Do you cast your magic from an evil place?"

The head on the statue tilted briefly to one side and the veil swung with the movement. "A dark place, most certainly, but that does not mean it is evil. As you said, there is a transference of magic upon the death of a mage to a newborn babe. Yet I possess power of a different sort that cannot be wielded by those who live."

Lady Gabriella's words from the previous day came back to him. The woman had commented on how the Miles family had fallen with the mage's death. That woman saw only the removal of society's privileges. What she did not see was how it also removed its strictures. The mage was no longer bound to work for the benefit of England. He found society's expectations could wrap a man in gilded chains. What would it be like to shake them off and stand free?

"Do you no longer serve England?" he asked.

"I serve a greater purpose in finding the French mage who created this curse. My Afflicted sisters only want their lives back, and yet you consider one of us capable of this terrible crime." The voice seemed to ride the undulations of the water and drift past him.

"I do not know what your sort are capable of. I only know what you require to sustain your Unnatural state." The Afflicted feasted on human brains. Once having overcome that taboo, who knew what other disgusting acts they were capable of committing?

"Hannah is a most able assistant to her father. I'm sure that if you asked, she would tell you what we have learned so far. Not all of it is detailed in reports sent to the Ministry of Unnaturals." Now she used a bird, flitting from tree to tree, to project her words.

Wycliff was forced to raise his head to find where it perched high above. It was difficult to reconcile the veiled creature speaking through a sparrow with the fierce mage who had once split the ground under a charging French regiment and sent more than a hundred men plunging straight to Hell. He could still hear the shrill cries of their horses, taken down with the riders.

He turned to regard her still form. What could such a creature do? "How can we ascertain what an Afflicted would do in a situation, when you hide behind veils and masks?"

The statue didn't move, even when she spoke. "The veil only obscures my physical appearance. It does not hide who I am. Shouldn't a person be judged on their actions, rather than on their name or outward appearance?"

He dug his short nails into his palms behind his back. He knew what they were. Dead. Abominations that should have been forcibly interred in graves and mausoleums. Some had the faint sweet scent of decay about them, or used cloves to mask the rot, but no such aromas wafted from Lady Miles. There was no quiet thud of a heart or inhalation of breath. She was invisible to his senses even though he saw her before him.

Until she turned her attention to him and the prickle raced over his skin.

She picked at the bleached linen of her skirt. It tumbled to the ground, even though her legs stopped above the knee. "I am fascinated that a man such as yourself should fall victim to the trap of perception. I expected more of you."

He stiffened. Talking to the dead mage was like making your way across a ravine via tightrope. One misstep and he would plunge to his death. "I don't know what you mean."

She huffed a gentle laugh that caused the gauzy veil to shiver. "You know exactly what I mean. We all have secrets, but the day approaches when you will have to confront yours."

He froze. She couldn't possibly know. No one did. He barely understood it himself, and he would not crawl on his belly to seek the help of those who could make sense of it. To do that, he would have to admit his greatest shame.

Lady Miles clasped white-gloved hands on her lap. From veil to dress and gloves, she was clothed in white. The rose behind her ear was the only touch of colour about her. She could have been a ghost, sent to torment him. "Your secret is yours to hide or reveal. But you are adrift on an unfamiliar ocean. You need to find an anchor before you are lost without hope of salvage."

"You mock me, Lady Miles." He let out a long, slow breath through his nose. Was she a mind reader? He fully intended to bury his secrets in the deepest, darkest pit he could find and ensure they never saw the light of day. He refused to use them even to speed his investigation, for to do that, he would have to unmask himself to all of society.

The bird fluttered down from the trees and rested on her outstretched hand. "On the contrary. I am trying to help another tortured soul through the long night we both must endure."

"I do not require any help, and I prefer that my secrets lie undisturbed."

"And does that help you sleep at night?" Both bird and mage seemed to peer through him.

"I shall await Miss Miles in the carriage. Good day, Lady Miles." He nodded and left, brushing foliage out of the way as he traversed the jungle back to the house.

## 10

Hannah didn't have time to change her gown, so her dark green cotton would have to suffice. At least the colour wouldn't show grass stains from being out in the garden, and her silk shawl would make it look more appropriate for paying calls. She undid her hair, smoothed it all back, and twisted it up again. Several pins secured it in place and then she plonked her bonnet on top to hide the lot. She tied the ribbons under her chin as she descended the stairs.

Mary stood at the bottom, wringing her hands and biting her lip.

"Whatever is the matter, Mary? Is it Mother?" She shouldn't have left her mother alone with the viscount, but surely a powerful mage was able to wrangle a petulant noble. Or perhaps Mother had turned him into an actual dark cloud and not a metaphorical one.

"Oh no, miss. It's *him*. He swept back through here in ever such a black mood and is waiting outside. I don't envy you, miss." Mary peered around Hannah at the closed front door as though she expected *him* to be summoned by her words.

Mother's storm had arrived after all, and had stuffed itself into a carriage. Would it be rattling with thunder and lightning when she emerged from the house?

Hannah patted Mary's hands. "Thank you. I shall have a most invigorating afternoon. Perhaps I should take Father's old sword cane in case I must make a quick defensive parry."

The maid snorted and then covered her mouth.

Out on the road, there was no sign of bolts exploding through the carriage windows. The viscount, however, did wear a stormy expression when Hannah climbed inside. His dark brows were drawn and his black eyes narrowed. Once again he stared at his timepiece as though it confirmed that Hannah had offended him further by making him wait.

"Where are we going today, my lord?" Hannah was determined to be polite in the face of his rudeness, but it did require monumental effort. The man almost begged to be snapped at, the way he glowered at everyone.

"The Knightley residence first, then the Talbots'." He rapped on the roof with his cane, then dropped the pocket watch back into its pocket on his waistcoat. He drummed his fingers on the carriage seat for a long minute. "You made the observation that a starving Afflicted would act differently. Are there other characteristics of an Afflicted in such a state?"

Hannah blinked at him. Had he just sought her knowledge on the subject? "A person in such a state is what others would refer to as *mad*. The hunger consumes them literally and figuratively. Their bodies begin to decay, and rot moves upward from the extremities. They are frenzied, tearing at themselves and often crying uncontrollably. The symptoms only abate when they are fed."

His hand curled into a fist as his body tensed. "Does it have to be human? Could they not subsist on cow or pig brains instead?"

Hannah remembered the poor women who tested other species' tissue, with disastrous results. "No. We found that substituting another species' brain did not halt the natural process of decay, although it did remove the worst of the craving. The disease is species dependent. For example, Afflicted mice require the brains of mice."

He exhaled through his nose and one by one, released his fingers from a tight grip. His words were measured, as though he sought to control them. "Is such a cannibalistic and murderous rage what lurks behind the veils and masks of all Afflicted?"

"You are disgusted by them," Hannah whispered. That was why he treated them so rudely and why he appeared to teeter on the verge of a violent outburst.

The hand curled into a fist again and he stared out the window. "They are not just Unnatural, they are inhuman, subsisting on the minds of decent Englishmen. They should be rounded up and burned so no trace of their blight remains on this earth." He bit the words out as though each syllable tasted bitter in his mouth.

His reaction not only stole Hannah's words, but also her ability to think. Her entire being froze in disbelief and she simply stared at him while the carriage swayed back and forth. Only when they hit a pothole in the road and she was jolted to one side did her mind recommence its operation. She wanted to yell at him, to accuse him of the most horrid preju-dice. She wanted to cry for all the Afflicted like her mother, who had been cruelly taken from their fami-lies in the prime of life.

"You would blame the women for their state? They were all, each and every one of them, victims of the foul weapon created by French mages. None sought the fate thrust upon them so cruelly." She clasped her hands together in her lap to stop the rage that shook them.

"They died. They should have the dignity to stay

that way." His nostrils flared and he enunciated each word slowly, as though he thought her dim-witted.

*Oh, let the storm break. How dared he!*

Anger flashed through Hannah and if she could have hurled a lightning bolt and skewered him to the seat, she would have. "What a cold life you must lead, that you would wish so many women a horrid end because of the actions of others. We are fortunate that most of the ensorcelled powder was destroyed and only three hundred containers made their way into the dressing rooms of noblewomen. Would you have a different opinion if tens of thousands of *men* had been infected by their *snuff habit?*"

His black eyes drilled into Hannah. "There are many challenges facing England. We waste resources keeping these creatures ambulatory. Great scientific minds should find subjects more worthy of their time —such as finding a way to stop more Unnatural creatures breaching the veil between our world and Hell."

Fury gave her the strength to meet his hellish gaze. She stiffened her spine and squared her jaw. "I am grateful for men like my father, who did not turn his back on the woman he loved simply because her pulse stopped. He works tirelessly to find a way to wrest her free of death's grip. I would consider myself *blessed* to ever find a man who loves so deeply. Which is obviously something you cannot comprehend." Hannah stared out the window and blinked back tears. Her father would fight until his last breath for her mother.

Viscount Wycliff grunted and proceeded to ignore her until the carriage stopped and the driver opened the door. The black cloud swept out and the driver jumped back, out of his way.

"Everything all right, miss?" he asked as he peered inside and held out a hand to assist her.

"Yes, thank you. I suspect his lordship swallowed something that did not agree with him."

Hannah took her time gathering her shawl about her shoulders, and looped the ends over her arms. Before her stretched a row of modest terrace houses. Each had an identical cast-iron railing along the front and leading up to the front door.

A startled maid, not a butler, held the door open for her. It appeared Wycliff had already stormed the parapets, as there was no sign of him in the hall.

"Hannah Miles to see Miss Emma Knightley, please." She couldn't hear raised voices or screams, which meant he hadn't yet started his interrogation.

"Lord Wycliff and Miss Knightley are this way, miss," the maid said as she gestured to a door to her left and closest to the front of the house.

The Knightley parlour reminded Hannah of the one in her family home. The decor was at least twenty years behind current fashion. The sofas were worn but comfortable looking and covered in a cheerful floral pattern. Books were piled on the end tables, waiting to be picked up and delved into. The room was tidy and clean, but with the relaxed shabbiness that comes from regular use.

Emma perched on a chaise and twisted her hands in her skirts. Her parents, a handsome couple somewhere in their fifties, held hands on the opposite chaise. Wycliff stood in the middle of the room, staring at Miss Knightley. For a moment it looked as though Hannah had stumbled upon a nervous suitor about to propose, the entire room on tenterhooks waiting for the words to be spoken.

Then she remembered that this was Wycliff and everyone was no doubt braced for the incoming cannonball.

Hannah edged around the viscount and murmured a greeting as she took the seat next to Emma. The poor woman needed some defence against Wycliff's barbs. The attack was launched just as Hannah sat.

"Did your fiancé call off the engagement because you died?" Wycliff asked.

Emma's hands stilled in her lap. "Yes. He disengaged himself to find a bride he could legally wed and who could present him with an heir—as he has every right to do. I believe he is most happy with his choice."

Hannah's heart broke for the other young woman. To think love was within your grasp, only to have it coldly snatched away. The French curse had revealed the fickleness of men. Women found themselves abandoned by those who had once professed undying love. It seemed men only remained true up until the point such affection was tested. What a sad statement about their society that men like her father, who continued to love a woman with no pulse, were the rare exceptions.

Hannah studied Viscount Wycliff. He seemed such an intense individual, one who should have the capacity to love a woman with constancy. What a shame that he seemed to be incapable of love for another.

The piercing stare remained fixed on Miss Knightley. "I understand that on the night of the ball, you were seen with a stain on your dress. Where is the garment?"

A gasp came from the older Knightleys and Emma's eyes widened. She turned to Hannah with an expression of complete betrayal, like a shivering puppy that had just been kicked out into the snow. Far from being her defender, Hannah had turned into her persecutor.

"It was red wine. I told you. You saw it," she whispered.

"I'm sorry. I had to tell the viscount what I saw." Guilt created a hollow void inside Hannah. How had Wycliff managed to flip their roles and make *her* the awful one in the room?

"Fetch the dress, Emma. That will satisfy the viscount, I am sure," her mother said.

The young woman nodded and leapt to her feet. She hurried from the room as though she couldn't wait to get away from Hannah the Horrid. Wycliff stalked to the window and stared out at the street with his hands clasped behind his back.

Mr Knightley bowed his head. "I shall never forgive myself." His muttered words broke the heavy silence.

"What can you not forgive?" Hannah asked.

Mrs Knightley sniffed and then dabbed at her eyes with a handkerchief. "All her friends spoke of the Russian émigré who had a limited amount of the amazing face powder used by the Tsarina. They all wanted some. They said it would give a woman a delicate complexion of the finest porcelain. She talked of nothing else for weeks and weeks, but it was so expensive—"

Mr Knightley squeezed his wife's hand and took up the narrative. "We acquired a jar for her birthday. Emma was overjoyed. Then one by one her friends fell ill, until one day, the French curse snatched our darling daughter too."

"I'm so sorry." Hannah looked around the room and thought how easily this life could have been hers. Both families were minor nobility who struggled to make ends meet. Two sets of loving parents would do anything for their only daughters. As she gathered her thoughts, other things registered in her mind. The unfaded shapes on the walls where paintings had been removed. Marks in the rugs made by the phantom feet of chairs. The lack of candlesticks, bookends, or ornaments on the shelves.

Emma returned with the gown draped over her arms and extended from her body as though trying to remove herself from it. Wycliff turned from the window and peered at the stain. A collection of dull brown dots and dribbles marred one portion of the satin. It could have been wine, gravy, or paint.

He picked up the section of fabric and sniffed. His nostrils flared as he drew a deep breath—and then he sneezed. "What have you covered this with?"

Emma crumpled the gown in her arms and clutched it to her chest. "A cleaning paste. I was hoping to wash the stain out, but it didn't work. I cannot remove it."

He grunted deep in his throat as he pulled forth a handkerchief and sneezed into it again. Whatever Emma had used on the stain worked better on the viscount than snuff.

"When did you last feed?" he asked as he waved away the gown.

From the sofa, Mrs Knightley made a horrified noise and lurched to one side in a dead faint. Mr Knightley caught her in his arms and lowered her so that she rested against the rolled arm.

The older gent glared at Wycliff. "Steady on, my lord, there is no need to be vulgar."

Therein lay one big difference between Emma's family and Hannah's. There was no fainting over feeding habits in the Miles household.

Wycliff arched a dark brow and *tsk*ed at the unconscious woman. "Your daughter is Afflicted. She has to feed to stave off the rot. Given that she exhibits very few symptoms apart from her pallor and lack of breathing, I assume she is well fed?"

Emma moved to stand between Wycliff and her parents. Her protective instincts had clearly been aroused and she used the treacherous dress as a shield. "My parents see to my needs and I have a monthly delivery from Unwin and Alder. You can confirm that with them if you wish. I assume there will be no more questions. You have disrupted our day quite enough."

He stared at the young woman for a long moment, then he spun on his heel and left.

Hannah rose, embarrassed at the role she had played in these events. "I am sorry. I do hope you can forgive me for telling him about the stain." She dropped a curtsey and followed the viscount out.

In other circumstances, if their paths had crossed, they might have become firm friends. Hannah suspected she had irreparably damaged such a possibility now. As she climbed into the waiting carriage, she wondered if there was any point in rebuking the viscount for being rude.

Again.

The man seemed oblivious. Society's disapproval was water off the duck's back and didn't affect him one bit. How could he rail against society's treatment of him while inflicting his own prejudices on others?

# 11

"It could be blood on her gown, but I could not tell. The cleaning paste had distorted its appearance and odour." Wycliff rapped on the roof and the carriage moved off.

Hannah would see to it that he didn't condemn Emma based on an indeterminate stain on her dress. "Or it could simply have been red wine or even gravy. I couldn't distinguish what it was and I saw it the night of the ball. And, need I remind you, I am well acquainted with the sight of bloodstains. Besides, Miss Knightley has loving parents who see to her hunger. She is remarkably untouched by her Affliction and is no starving specimen."

Black eyes drilled through Hannah and made her squirm on the seat. "What will they do when they have sold all the furnishings? How will they pay her monthly account then, to ensure she doesn't rot on her feet?"

Ah. She wasn't the only one who had noticed the missing effects. The impact on families such as the Knightleys made it all the more imperative that her father find a cure. If the Afflicted women could be wrested back from death, they could go on to live normal lives. Women like Emma could marry and present their parents with grandchildren to love and dote upon.

"I do not know, my lord. Perhaps they will sell the house and move to rented lodgings? Some parents will go to extraordinary lengths for their children." Hers would. Never for a second did she have cause to doubt what her parents would do for her. "Would you condemn Miss Knightley because at some time in the future she *might* fall behind in her account with Unwin and Alder?"

He made that rough noise in the back of his throat and stared out the window. For some reason it reminded her of a dog's growl and conjured to mind her mother's comment about finding her a dog for company.

*Please don't let it be a foul-tempered hound like this one.*

The carriage swayed over the cobbled streets and Hannah let the movement soothe her mood and carry her thoughts soaring over the rooftops. She was so used to silence between them that the viscount's next words caught her off guard.

"Does it make any difference whether the Afflicted ingest the brains of those who carry a trace of magic from a mage ancestor, or those from an ordinary person?"

"Pardon?" Hannah took a moment to pull her thoughts back from where they had scattered themselves across the sky.

When she looked across the carriage, for once his face seemed relaxed when he spoke to her, his eyebrows at ease and not duelling one another. If he smiled, he might even be considered handsome.

"The curse was created by French mages," he said. "I wondered if feeding on the minds of those with magic in their blood might somehow alleviate or affect the symptoms differently."

Hannah stared at him. It was a genius hypothesis and one that had not occurred to either her or her father. They had studied the difference that species of brain made, and fresh brains versus a number of preserved states, but they had not considered the particular *type* of organ within their own species. "I don't know. We have never pursued that line of enquiry."

"Perhaps it is not relevant." He turned back to the passing traffic out the window.

"No, it's not that. It is simply a question we

haven't postulated. I admit we have so much to learn about the Afflicted we are sometimes struggling in the dark seeking a light to guide our way." She worried her father would work himself into an early grave trying to find a cure. Hannah alleviated his burden as much as possible, but more men were needed to investigate a cure, to spread the load that consumed their family.

Lord Wycliff met her gaze and the open, interested look stayed on his face. She took the lack of disapproval as encouragement to expand her ideas.

"We know so little of how the physiology of a mage's descendants—the aftermages—differs from that of an ordinary human. For example, does magic reside in their mind, their blood, or their soul? And flowing from that, could consuming magic relieve the effects of the dark magic the French inflicted upon these women?" Hannah's mind was abuzz with possibilities.

While it might not be a cure, what if ingesting natural magic bestowed some resistance to the rot? Then she considered her mother's condition—being a mage had not offered any respite from the symptoms. Or did magic have to be consumed? That, of course, would create a horrible side effect in an increased demand for the bodies of those with mage blood in their veins. They would have to maintain secrecy in any such study.

His lips quirked upward for a brief moment in what could almost be mistaken for an attempt at a smile. The effect was quite devastating and stole Hannah's breath. Then the brows narrowed again and she was released from his spell. "Unwin and Alder are required to keep records of what they supply to the Afflicted. If they also record the names of the donors, it would allow you to ascertain which are the magically gifted descendants of mages. With that information, you could implement such a study."

Hannah couldn't wait to discuss this new idea with her parents. They would have to consult the mage genealogies, a task her mother could undertake. Then they could cross reference those with records of donors and divide the Afflicted into groups to study. "This could be groundbreaking. We could have one group supplied with magically gifted minds, one with ordinary, and one with an even mix of the two. I must consult with Father so we can get this underway as soon as possible."

His lips quirked in that all too brief smile again, then his attention drifted out the window.

There was one more thing Hannah had to do. The words almost stuck in her throat and she had to try three times to spit them out. "Thank you, my lord, for this most excellent idea."

He huffed, but at least it wasn't a growl this time.

The carriage took them the short distance to the Talbot residence. Wycliff actually waited for her on the pavement and held out his hand. Hannah touched his glove as she stepped down, then he walked beside her to the front door. He was positively civilised.

It couldn't last.

The butler showed them through to a parlour with deep red and cream walls, whitewashed floors, and striped sofas. Lady Talbot continued the theme of red and cream with a gown that appeared to be made of a fabric inspired by the wallpaper. She had a short and curvaceous form, and her dark hair was peppered with grey and tucked up under a cap.

She wore no veil or mask, nor did she employ a fan. That wasn't conclusive as to the state of her pulse though. Decay might not have blemished Lady Talbot's outward appearance, just as Emma Knightley remained free of visible signs. Some women were fortunate in being infected last and therefore had the benefit of prompt access to *pickled cauliflower* to keep the rot at bay.

Lady Talbot laced her hands together and gestured to a chaise opposite. Her gaze darted to Wycliff, who prowled the outer edges of her parlour, and back to Hannah. "Please be seated, Miss Miles, Lord Wycliff."

Wycliff waved away her offer. "What were your movements the night of the Loburn engagement ball?"

Lady Talbot smiled at Hannah and then spoke to a cushion next to her, unable to meet Lord Wycliff's piercing eyes. "I only danced one or two sets. I much prefer to catch up with my friends and watch the young people. It was quite a delightful evening and Miss Miles, your mother's magical gift was simply bewitching."

"It was charming, with the crystal butterflies and their music. But Lady Elizabeth was the star of the evening. She will make a most beautiful bride, don't you agree?" Hannah gathered her thoughts and fell into the easy patter of light conversation.

"Oh, yes. Such a handsome couple." Lady Talbot's hands fidgeted with the fringe on the cushion.

Hannah reviewed what little she knew of Lady Talbot. She had married at least fifteen years previously and was in her forties. She had ably performed her marital duties by providing the necessary heir and a spare before indulging herself with a daughter. She could have suffered the cursed plague and kept the protection of her husband. Not all lords took the opportunity to set aside older wives for younger versions. Some men had genuine affection for the mothers of their children and kept up the appearance of the wife still being alive.

Wycliff paced in front of the fireplace like a caged beast. Then he spun and pinned the older woman with a black glare. "Does your husband know about your lover or do you try, none too successfully, to keep him a secret?"

Hannah was struck dumb for the second time

that day. Lady Talbot looked on the verge of apoplexy. Her face turned a deeper shade of crimson than the burgundy drapes. Her eyes widened and she puffed in and out like a fat lap dog who has chased a rabbit for miles.

At length, she managed to draw a gulping breath. Then she raised a hand and pointed a finger at Wycliff's head. "How dare you! My affairs are most decidedly none of your business."

"We're done here. Come, Miss Miles." With that, he strode from the room.

Hannah blinked, wondering what on earth had just occurred. She had been warned the man was rude, had seen him ride roughshod over a number of ladies already, but to deliberately insult a member of the *ton* was beyond the pale. She rose on shaky legs and dropped an even shakier curtsey to the other woman. "Thank you so much for your time this after-noon, Lady Talbot. I can only offer the most sincere apology for Lord Wycliff's behaviour. He is most keen to solve the murder that blighted Lady Eliza-beth's announcement, and that makes him rather abrupt."

"And I am sorry for you, Miss Miles. What crime are you being punished for, that you must endure his company?" She peered over Hannah's shoulder, as though making sure the *he* in question did not return.

"I'm not sure what affront I committed to be so burdened, but it does seem to be my lot in life to apologise in his wake." There was a distressing regularity to the way these interviews played out. Ladies would admit them. Lord Wycliff would insult them. Hannah would try to repair the damage he inflicted.

No wonder Lady Loburn and Sir Manly Powers had insisted that a young lady accompany the viscount on his interviews. Someone had to do all the apologising.

Lord Wycliff waited in the carriage, his fingers drumming against his cane. A gentleman would have waited on the pavement for Hannah and offered her a hand into the carriage. How odd that, given all she had seen of the vile man, she still expected him to behave like a gentleman.

Hannah took her seat and glared at him. If she were a mariner, Wycliff would be the albatross around her neck. How would she ever be free of him? Admittedly, he had suggested the brilliant idea of studying the types of brains the Afflicted consumed, but that didn't make up for his behaviour.

She couldn't wait for the interviews to be over so she might never see his face again. No matter how handsome the lines of his profile, they didn't soften the ugliness on the inside. "There was no need to be deliberately rude to Lady Talbot."

"At the Loburn ball I saw Lady Talbot in the intimate embrace of a man who was not her husband." He rapped on the roof of the carriage and it moved off. Then he set the cane aside and reached into his jacket pocket for the list and pencil.

Hannah stared at her strange companion. The man lacked even the most fundamental understanding of how to behave in polite society. Had he even been raised in proper company? Or, as she suspected, had the young boy simply been left in the dog kennel to fight over scraps? "There was no need to call attention to her indiscretion."

He looked up and arched one black brow, a quizzical look on his face. "She blushed."

"You stormed out because she *blushed*?" The woman had looked positively on the verge of an apoplexy and it was lucky she hadn't had to restart her heart—

Oh. The clues clanged together in her mind. However had she missed it?

"The Afflicted are dead. As such they have no pulse, and their hearts do not beat. It is scientifically impossible for one of the Afflicted to blush, as you should be well aware. Therefore our interview was concluded." He flicked open the sheet of names and crossed one off in his bold hand.

All her life, Hannah had given her elders and betters respect. She did as she was told and never spoke out of turn. She held her silence no matter how provoked. Or she had—until she had the misfortune to cross paths with Viscount Wycliff. Since being forced into his company, she had witnessed him humiliate women with no regard for the poor creatures' suffering. He had forcibly stated his opinion that the unfortunate Afflicted should be rounded up and burned alive. Or burned dead. No, that wasn't right, either. Well, bother the semantics—he wanted to inflict upon them a torturous ending by fire.

Hannah Miles had, quite frankly, had enough.

"I am curious, my lord. Do you possess a natural talent for cruelty, or have you practiced for many years to perfect the verbal barbs that you inflict on those less fortunate than yourself?"

At first she wondered if he had heard her. He remained motionless. Then his head turned and his black eyes fixed on her.

He glared at her for such a long time that Hannah longed to look away or to disappear into the cracks between the cushions. But there was no escape. Having commenced this line of attack, she must stay the course. She would not show cowardice to this hellhound. Yes, that description fit him—he was a dog sent from Hell to vex her. She dug her nails into her palms to keep her gaze fixed on his.

His nostrils flared and reminded her of a bull just before it charged. Had she made him so very angry? Good. He deserved it for his thoughtless treatment of the late Lady Albright, Miss Emma Knightley, and Lady Talbot.

Then he rapped on the roof of the carriage with his cane.

Hannah's stomach lurched as they jolted to a sudden stop.

Wycliff leaned forward, his weight resting on the silver cap of his cane. "I assure you, Miss Miles, cruelty was a lesson I learned at the hands of society. I returned from the war to find I had been judged *in absentia* and sentenced to perdition."

Having said his piece, he flung open the door and stepped from the carriage to disappear into the bustle of people on the pavement.

Well, that settled it. She just had to find out what had happened to him on the Peninsula.

## 12

Wycliff abandoned the carriage before he wrapped his hands around Miss Miles's neck and throttled her. Anger was a wild beast inside him that demanded a release. Better he walk until it settled down within him.

Before he did something foolish, like kiss the woman to silence her biting remarks.

Her words were a stiletto through the ribs and straight into a vital organ. She was just like every other shallow woman in society—judging him when they knew nothing about him or what he endured.

His body rocked to an abrupt halt as though he had run into an invisible wall. His imagination conjured the linen-draped image of Lady Miles before him, admonishing him for judging her based on her disturbing outward appearance. Then the image morphed into an angry Miss Miles, accusing him of blaming the Afflicted for their state. But the words that resounded most inside him were that she would consider herself blessed to ever find a man who loved so deeply that he would battle death for her.

Poppycock and nonsense.

He waved his hand and the image returned to the shadows in his mind. What use did he have for love? What he needed was a ready source of cash. His estate in Dorset was bankrupt and creditors were banging on his (rented) door. To have any hope of rebuilding his ancestral home, he needed the income offered by Sir Manly as his investigator. An heiress would put him back on a steady keel, if he could stomach the idea of taking a wife purely for financial gain.

Returning to the task at hand, Wycliff pulled the small notebook from his pocket. He had transferred the list of names to the book and one by one, the list of suspects was whittled down. Today he would tackle a different angle on the murder. He walked briskly to the business district with its large warehouses. Laden carts drawn by heavy horses took loads to smaller retailers.

He made for a warehouse that stood apart from the others. It was segregated by a strip of dirt, bereft of even the hardiest plant in the available space, as though even grass and weeds wouldn't grow close to its walls.

A small sign over the door proclaimed it the warehouse of Unwin and Alder. The business founders were perfect examples of criminals who had built a legitimate occupation. The two men were former resurrectionists who used to supply doctors and medical students with illegally obtained bodies. Now they were government-sanctioned suppliers to the Afflicted of what was politely referred to as *pickled cauliflower*. As the only legal operatives, their business was booming as they serviced their captive market.

No working-class carts pulled away from this warehouse. Their wares were discreetly packaged in plain boxes like those used by millinery shops and delivered by a man who resembled a doorman delivering a lady's purchases.

Wycliff pulled open the front door of their office. Within, it looked like a solicitor's rooms, with dark panelled wood and warm rugs underfoot. Only its location among the other warehouses, instead of a more prestigious high-street address, gave a hint as to its indelicate nature.

A secretary sat at the front desk and scribbled, the quill waving back and forth with each breath he took. He looked up over the top of gold-rimmed spectacles and squinted at Wycliff. "May I help you, sir?"

Women didn't cross this threshold unless they were in desperate need. Orders were placed by trusted footmen, and then husbands or sons bore the responsibility of paying for the goods. The invoice shuffled among those for bonnets, ribbons, and shoes.

"I wish to speak to either Unwin or Alder on a most urgent matter." He hated dealing with underlings, and this one wouldn't have access to the records he required. Layers of secrecy concealed the more gruesome details of the Afflicted's condition from the rest of England.

Their existence on this earth shouldn't be extended, regardless of who they were related to. If the plague had struck the working class, Parliament would have dispatched the army to deal with them and the Afflicted would have been eradicated in short order. But because a small number of ladies of the *ton* were infected, a whole new industry had sprung up to service their needs. They needed veils, expensive porcelain masks, pomanders and, more disturbingly, *pickled cauliflower.*

The clerk set down his quill and adjusted his spectacles while making put-out *harumphs* in the back of his throat. Wycliff cut him off before he marshalled his petty administrative power.

Wycliff crossed his arms and stared at his fingernails. "I am Viscount Wycliff, investigator for the Ministry of Unnaturals. Unwin and Alder can either talk to me or their license to practice will be revoked. I can have you shut down by the end of the day."

The man's mouth snapped shut and his eyes

narrowed further. But he could bluster all he wanted. Wycliff wasn't moving.

The clerk blew out a resigned sigh. "One moment, my lord."

He unwound his gangly frame from the chair and slipped through a set of double doors behind his desk. Voices rose and fell beyond and then the clerk reappeared. "Mr Unwin would be delighted to field your concerns." He gestured to the now open doorway.

Wycliff strode through and snapped the doors shut behind him, in case the clerk thought to follow. Let him press his ear to the door if he wished to know Wycliff's business.

Unwin rose from behind his enormous desk. He had the look of a man grown soft on easy living. A florid face had the distinctive red nose of one who enjoyed his brandy and plenty of it. His waistline expanded just as his company's bottom line improved. It had been a long time since he had done physical labour with a shovel under cover of darkness, or had to run from those protecting the sanctity of the churchyards.

He plastered a smile on his face. "Lord Wycliff, how may I assist you?"

"I am investigating the murder at the Marquess of Loburn's home." He jumped straight to the matter. He wasn't here to exchange pleasantries. Life would be more efficient if everyone cut out the small talk.

The man nodded and clasped his hands behind his back. "Oh? Terrible matter, I am sure, but what brings you to my door?"

Wycliff paused for a moment as irritation grew in his breast. Sir Manly had advised him to curb his quick temper, but men like Unwin sorely tested his resolve. "Don't play coy with me. I believe the perpetrator of the heinous crime is one of the Afflicted. Who else would scoop out the poor man's brains? I want to know whom you supply, who is behind in their payments, and whether anyone has missed a delivery."

As the man swallowed, his Adam's apple bobbed up and down. It wasn't easy to cloak his business in respectability. The taint of murder might make Londoners look askance at his operation. "Surely you don't suspect one of our clients?"

The man seemed as slow as molasses. "No. I suspect a hungry Afflicted who is *no longer* one of your clients. Where do you keep your records?"

Unwin's face grew redder and he swallowed again as though suddenly thirsty. "Those records are strictly confidential, Lord Wycliff. Those poor ladies—"

Enshrined in the Unnaturals Act was the edict that such creatures must uphold English law. The Afflicted forgot they were dead, and as such, had no rights or protection other than what their money could purchase. "The dead have no rights to privacy. The records?"

The man paled. Just as his clientele were in the highest ranks of society, it also meant he would have equally highly placed enemies should they find out he had handed over their names.

"I cannot," he gasped, like a dying man needing water.

"Which will inconvenience your clients more... my knowing their names, or your business closing its doors?" Wycliff threw the man onto the horns of a dilemma. Which damage was worse—lost reputation or lost revenue?

It took Unwin mere seconds to make up his mind. "If you would follow me, please, my lord."

Just as he suspected. Unwin would rather lose the records than the income.

The large man led the way from the room, across the main outer office and through a smaller door that opened onto a dim corridor. A skylight above was covered with metal bars and was the only source of light. The sun was filtered through opaque glass that cast thick lines on the hardwood floor.

One side of the corridor had three large metal doors, such as Wycliff would expect to find in a bank. No noise filtered through the thick walls, but a faint metallic whiff, underlaid with something sharp like vinegar, made him wrinkle his nose. The absence of windows and metal walls couldn't completely erase all trace of evidence that the warehouse dealt in death.

At the end of the corridor was a smaller door, made of oak and oiled to a dark stain. Unwin withdrew a key chain from his pocket and fitted a shiny brass key into the lock. As he turned the key, the hollow *clunk* echoed down the hallway. He paused with his hand on the lever and glanced over his shoulder at Wycliff. The former grave robber hesitated before pushing open the door.

This time they stepped into a darkened storeroom that carried the sharp tang of preservatives. Once again there were no external windows, only a barred skylight above. The opaque glass allowed light to filter through but stopped the curious from pressing their noses up close to see what happened below. The room was cloaked in an eternal twilight that added to the eerie atmosphere. Neat metal shelves marched in rows across the room. Shelves held glass jars containing the pickled contents.

Wycliff pinched his nose as the sharp odour stabbed up into his brain. He tried not to think too long about the origins of the pale slices suspended in liquid. However, his curiosity was roused when a stolen glance showed the liquids to be different colours and densities.

"Why do they not all appear the same?" He gestured to two rows in particular. The top shelf seemed to house its contents in a clear liquid while those on the shelf below had a red tinge with what appeared to be specks of dirt floating in it.

"Each lady has a personal preference. Some like a touch of rosemary or other herbs to flavour the vinegar. Some Afflicted prefer that particular types of alcohol be used as a preservative. We have developed a number of different recipes to relieve the *ennui* of a monotonous diet." Unwin gestured toward the orderly rows, but his fingers stopped several inches from the glass.

Wycliff sucked in his disgust, as bitter as the tart air in the storeroom. He held tight to Miss Miles's words that the women did not choose to be so cursed. But that didn't excuse the man who desecrated the poor deceased to pander to the tastes of the wealthy undead. Perhaps, like monks, they should consider their *monotonous diet* penance for what they consumed.

"Are none whole?" Despite all he had seen on the battlefield, he was relieved that nothing was identifiable. It soothed his mind to think he looked at nothing more than sliced brassica.

The merchant peered at one jar, where the label announced the slices drifted in brandy, sweetened with peaches and cinnamon. "No. Each is pre-sliced into thirty pieces, or one month's supply. Some make it last six weeks by alternating a whole slice with a half. This way, the lady does not have to handle the matter any more than absolutely required. They only have to spear a piece with a long-handled fork."

"Do the poor families know what has become of their relatives?" Wycliff wondered aloud as he waved an arm at the rows of large jars.

"The common folk are amply paid for the minor diversion of their loved one out of the way to their final resting place. Our men are quick and efficient. We can harvest what we require and have the body back in less than two hours. To explain the stitches in the scalp, they are told the bodies are required for a phrenology study." Unwin sounded just like a businessman making a speech to his investors, but he stopped short of mentioning the lucrative returns.

"A phrenology study that requires the scalp to be removed? I assume payment silences any concerns." In one of the rooms behind its thick metal door, the required organ was removed. Did people question what happened in those two hours, or were they willfully blind? When you subsisted on the brink of poverty, a handful of coins went a long way toward allaying fears about what had gone missing from a daughter, uncle, or cousin.

Unwin huffed a quiet snort. "Do you really think the people of England want to know what goes on here and what exactly a handful of the posh ladies are nibbling on for supper?"

It was a British trait to make the best of a bad situation by dressing it up as something else. People didn't want to know that a small group of undead ladies of the *ton* were feasting on the brains of the common folk. It was a more palatable tale to say that women afflicted with a magical French curse needed pickled cauliflower to allow them to continue as upstanding members of society. Just don't ask where the cauliflower was grown.

"But it crosses a line when one decides to crack a fellow's head open during a ball." The small number of Afflicted were tolerated so long as they obeyed society's laws and didn't covet the brains of the still living.

"Quite." They left the room, and Unwin carefully locked the door behind him. He then walked to another door, this one made of the same wood and design as the previous one. He selected a different key from the chain attached to his waistcoat button. The lock clanged as it drew back and then he pushed inside.

The next room was wrapped in complete darkness. Leaving the door open to allow a dim shaft of light, he grabbed a tinderbox from a nearby table, lit a lantern, and turned up the wick. He set the lantern on the table. Two walls of this room were made up of small wooden drawers. They reminded Wycliff of shelves in a mausoleum.

Unwin gestured to the multitude of drawers. "This is where we keep a record of each lady's order. The cards will tell you the date of each delivery, the type of cauliflower dispatched, and payments made."

"How are they arranged?" Wycliff cast an eye over the numerous drawers and did a quick count. There were fifteen drawers in a vertical row, and twenty across, making a total of three hundred small drawers. How many Afflicted were there exactly, and how many minds had they collectively consumed to stave off the rot eating at their flesh? All so they could continue to tread the floors at Almack's or pay visits to one another to indulge in shallow chatter.

"Alphabetical, my lord. One drawer per customer, although not all the drawers are in use. We only mark the initial of the last name on the drawer." Unwin pulled open the nearest drawer with the letter *D* on the outside. Within were a series of handwritten cards with notes and financial transactions.

"Do you note the name of the person who provided the cauliflower that makes up each delivery?"

Unwin frowned and his eyes squinted almost closed. "I don't understand, my lord?"

"I have discussed with Miss Miles, the daughter of Sir Hugh Miles, the leading researcher into the Afflicted, if it makes any difference whether they ingest the brains of the aftermages or those of ordinary folk. You have the records to enable that study."

"Whether it makes a difference?" Unwin

produced a handkerchief and mopped his brow, as though he found the conversation taxing.

Wycliff opened one drawer and peered at the tightly packed cards within. "To their symptoms. Do the Afflicted improve if they ingest matter from an aftermage?"

The other man's eyes widened, then he practically salivated at the potential. "Good Lord. We could charge a premium for the aftermage brains if they are more effective. Of course we shall cooperate in any way we can in such an inquiry."

Wycliff held in his disgust at the open greed on Unwin's face at the thought of lining his pockets even further. "I would suggest that you immediately begin to record who receives which brain. It shouldn't be too difficult. Assuming your staff can count, I would suggest assigning a number to each harvested mind and then recording that number on the Afflicted's delivery sheet. An examination of the mage genealogies will tell us who is an aftermage among your 'pickled cauliflowers.'"

"A brilliant suggestion, my lord. I will instruct my staff directly and ensure we begin recording the required details. We can even hold back new stock until we identify whether or not they are aftermages, so we can more accurately facilitate a study of effects."

"I won't hold you up. I have much to do." He would begin by reviewing the names on his list. A quick cross reference to Unwin and Alder's cards would tell him who was, or wasn't, Afflicted. Then he could focus on payment and delivery dates.

Particularly those of Emma Knightley and how her parents managed to pay her bill.

**13**

Hannah burst through the door and draped the staircase newel post with her bonnet and shawl. Then she made a beeline for the small, discreet door in the wooden panelling that led down to her father's laboratory.

The temperature dropped as the darkened stairs took her down into the earth. Her mother had had the rooms dug deep into the ground not to store wine or preserves, but to take advantage of the cooler temperature for Sir Hugh's work. The solid stone walls had no windows and this far below the house, there was little fear of anything escaping and going on a rampage in London.

Her father had three rooms down here. One was the autopsy or examination room, dominated by the large stone table. Another was the workspace that ran the width of the house, with its long benches and rows of shelves with their specimens. The third room was Sir Hugh's private study and his consultation room.

The stairs ended in a short, wide corridor that was large enough to manoeuvre a body on a hand cart. Hannah chose the door to the workroom and found her father seated at the long bench, peering at a specimen under his microscope.

"We need to study the *type* of brains," she burst out. Like a kettle letting off steam, she was relieved to finally unburden herself of the ideas building in her head.

Her father peered at her over the rims of his spectacles. "We did—mouse, cow, pig, and sheep. None worked, except they made the ladies less aware of the damage done to them."

Hannah waved her hands. "No. Types of *human* brains—aftermages or ordinary. Lord Wycliff asked whether ingesting the brain of an aftermage made any difference to the French curse. I believe we must answer that question at once."

Her father's grey eyebrows jumped and he let out a low exclamation. He took off his spectacles and placed them on the bench. "I say, what an idea. We haven't looked at it from that angle."

"I know." Hannah grabbed her apron off the hook by the door and dropped it over her head. She tied a bow in the ends behind her back as she approached the workbench. "Imagine if consuming the brain of an aftermage somehow counteracted the French magic and alleviated the symptoms."

Sir Hugh rubbed his chin as his mind turned over the possibilities. "Conversely, magic added to magic might magnify the curse and speed the decay. Sera's power did not stop the curse's spread through her limbs."

"Oh, I hadn't considered that." Some of Hannah's excitement deflated. She wouldn't want to make the Afflicted women worse.

Sir Hugh patted her hand. "What do I always say, Hannah?"

"Hypothesise, then strategise." She needed the reminder of her father's motto. They wouldn't know what effect, if any, the difference might make until they conducted a study and analysed the results. Then they could determine whether they needed to change the way they treated the Afflicted. She didn't want to think about the possible long-term effect of sparking a surge in demand for a particular type of brain.

Sir Hugh pulled a padded leather stool out from under the bench. "It is a fascinating idea. I assume there is some record kept of official donations to our cause?"

Were such conversations, Hannah wondered, why she had few social engagements? She would rather discuss which working-class people had surrendered their brains to feed the nobles than how to raise funds for a new fountain in the town square.

She sat on the stool and swung her legs under the bench. "Viscount Wycliff said Unwin and Alder are required to keep records of donations and deliveries. It will involve some hard work, but with their cooperation, we will be able to conduct such a study. I thought we might use three groups—one receiving donations from aftermages, one ordinary, and one an equal mix."

Sir Hugh pinched the bridge of his nose while he bowed his head in thought. "The problem will be establishing a baseline of an Afflicted's condition. We don't want to alert them to the nature of the study, but we require some way to know if their symptoms alter."

Hannah picked up a pencil and began making notes on a sheet of paper. "Perhaps, if the Ministry of Unnaturals agrees, we could say it is part of a study to reach out to all Afflicted and determine their current state? It is certainly no falsehood to say we want to investigate the long-term effects of the curse, and we can only do that by periodically reviewing the level of decay and comparing it against the previous examination."

Hannah added *Request permission from Sir Manly Powers* to her list. Having the Ministry sanction their work would smooth some of the bumps in the road ahead. Particularly the large mounds created by Viscount Wycliff, as he dug metaphorical holes in parlours around London.

"Excellent work, Hannah. While I cannot predict what we may find, I do hope we finally have the breakthrough we so desperately need to help these poor women."

They both fell silent for a long moment. The Affliction consumed many lives. Not only the women concerned, but their families as well. Thinking of families brought the day's interviews to mind.

"Today I saw Miss Emma Knightley, who is in remarkable condition, with no visible signs of decay. She even breathes, although it must take quite a sustained effort to keep it up." Hannah added more tasks to her growing list.

Sir Hugh took the sample off the microscope and replaced it with another. "Really? Do you know what she is feeding upon? There may be something in her particular diet or environment that is slowing her symptoms. Do you think she would allow me to examine her?"

Hannah doubted Emma Knightley wanted to see her, or any member of her family, in the near future. Although perhaps with time the young woman might forget Hannah's betrayal in telling Lord Wycliff about her gown. "I think not. The interview today was particularly horrid."

Sir Hugh's face fell. "Oh. There are, unfortunately, plenty of other Afflicted women for us to examine. Once we have the relevant records, your mother can delve into the genealogies to determine who among the donors is an aftermage. We should also record what generation they belong to, to see if that is another factor."

More notes were made. Hannah could see her days becoming full rather quickly. "We shall have to visit Unwin and Alder and establish a working relationship with their staff."

Sir Hugh picked up the delicate spectacles and returned them to his nose. Then he peered into the eyepieces of the microscope. "I'll leave it to you to sort out the details. You're much better at that than I."

Which meant Hannah remembered to sort such details. Sir Hugh had a tendency to become overly involved in his work and forget the time. Or the day. Hannah and Mary had to make sure he emerged at least once a day for a meal and to experience a little daylight.

"Did you determine anything about the unfortunate heart?" Hannah scanned the rows of bottles on the shelves adjacent to the bench. A variety of body parts and smaller mammals floated in preservative. While there were a few hearts, she didn't see the rotten one.

Sir Hugh continued to switch samples and divide his attention between Hannah and whatever was between the layers of glass. "No. It was quite beyond saving. I did discover that the advanced rot originated in the heart and spread outward, eating away the surrounding tissue. If the poor woman hadn't fallen down, she would have dissolved from the inside before much longer."

Hannah screwed up her face. What a terrible fate—to rot from the inside out until you simply collapsed in a puddle of fluids. "That is the opposite of the way decay usually progresses in the Afflicted. We have found it starts with the exterior, in the extremities, and then works upward and inward."

He looked up, excitement a sparkle in his eyes. Sir Hugh had two great passions in life—his wife, and his study to restart her heart. "Yes, quite a puzzle, is it not? Why did the French curse take such a different route in this poor woman? So far the only factor in play is the age of the powder."

"How do the mice fare?" Hannah glanced at the wall where the shelves held cages in a variety of sizes. One shelf held the mice who lived short, cursed lives. Large red tags with the letter *A* identified their cages. A blue tag with a number referenced other details of their Affliction. The shelf above was home to the healthy mice, who bred the donors for their Afflicted kin.

He huffed and shook his head. "Far too early to tell. I have infected three and we shall see what unfolds. I want to wait and see if they simply fall down like our poor maid."

That had taken six months. Hannah felt uncomfortable wishing the mice a quicker demise. Waiting was the worst part of scientific study, but knowledge revealed itself in its own time.

"Why don't you confer with your mother? You'll find her in the library today." Her father nudged her when she had been silent for too long.

She was finding it difficult to concentrate after her time with Lord Wycliff. Like a whirlwind, he uprooted her thoughts and hurled them in different directions. She needed quiet time with her mother to allow everything to settle down. "Do you need me this afternoon?"

He tapped her list of tasks. "Nothing I can't manage. The sooner you gather the records for your mother, the sooner we can begin our new study."

"Very well." She laid a hand on his shoulder and then removed her apron and hung it back on its hook. By the time Hannah slipped out the door, her father was once again engrossed in his research.

Back up the stairs she went, until she emerged in the subdued daylight of the entrance hall. Hannah set off along the corridor to the corner of the house that held the library. The house was enormous for just the three of them, with many twists and turns and more rooms than they could ever use. Her parents had hoped to fill it with the laughter of many children, a dream that was dashed when the Fates had only gifted them one child.

And then had come the Affliction.

Hannah paused with her fingers curled around the handle of the library door. While as the direct offspring of a mage she was devoid of any magical ability, she was still sensitive to it. Goosebumps washed up her arm, a sign that warned of magic being performed beyond the door. At times she lived in a constant state of alert, as her mother cast spells in the turret high above them and the prickling sensation rained down on Hannah.

Hannah pushed into the room she loved the most. Could there be anything more marvellous in the world than a library? Other women might prefer a ballroom, or a millinery shop, but Hannah swooned over books.

The square room was double height, with the floor above the library being her mother's turret room. Nearly all four walls were floor-to-ceiling bookshelves. Books barely allowed space for the large window, with the shelves rejoining above the frame to carry on their way.

Her parents had a shared devotion to books and the library perfectly merged magic and science. Tomes on a vast range of subjects were crammed into every shelf. Science books huddled together on one wall, magical volumes whispered to one another on a third. Fiction separated the two and the whole created a scene that soothed Hannah's fractious nerves and settled her mind after her morning with Wycliff.

Her mother sat at the huge desk with the window behind her. Today a delicate pearl and diamond tiara secured her heavy veil. Clad in her usual bleached linen and muslin, she resembled a bride waiting to meet her groom.

Hannah's shoes sank into the heavy rug as she walked to her mother's side and kissed her covered cheek. "What are you about today? The tiara usually means you are in a whimsical mood."

Seraphina raised a hand gloved in cotton to tap the pearl that hung, suspended, in the centre of the tiara. "I love this piece and since I no longer attend balls or the theatre, I have decided that at least one day a week will be a tiara day."

Hannah smiled. Despite all that had happened to her, her mother found some way to create a little joy or happiness in each day.

"I also dream of the day my daughter will wear it for her wedding." Seraphina took Hannah's hand.

An emptiness opened inside of Hannah. She would relish every moment of Lizzie's wedding, but there would never be such an event in her future. "Mother, please don't. You know why that can never happen."

The mage held Hannah's hand to her cheek.

"Allow your mother to dream, dearest. After all, I do believe in magic."

It would take more miracle than magic for her ever to see Hannah walk down the aisle. But she would allow her mother to dream. She turned her attention to the work before her. Spread out on the desk was a detailed map of France. Five wooden pillars sat at various points in the countryside, making five points of a star. Tiny, ghostly people who seemed made of ash stood in a small cluster in the centre of the star.

"What am I seeing?" Hannah asked. "I assume the five pillars are the French mages?"

"Yes. I have decided to tackle our quest from a different angle. I intend to locate the French mage who created this curse. If we know how he worked his original spell, then we could reverse it."

Hannah's hand hovered over the miniature ash people. "Does this small group have something to do with how you will accomplish that?"

"This curse was not sprung upon us untested. The French have their own Afflicted. Sir Ewan Shaw was shot on the battlefield by a French officer whom he said smelled of death. He found the same odour attached to the cache of face powder and snuff he discovered. I believe that French officer was Afflicted."

Ewan Shaw was a lycanthrope with a keen sense of smell—one of the original Highland Wolves.

While on a mission in Kent he had uncovered the French plot to release thousands of contaminated containers upon the English people.

"Imagine what would have happened if he hadn't found and destroyed all the infected powder," Hannah said as she stared at the map.

Seraphina waved a hand over the map and the ash people shrank even smaller, until they resembled ants. "Mass panic would have ensued and who knows how many would have died or been turned into secondary Afflicted. We are fortunate only two barrels of powder were mixed up by the smugglers and the curse was somewhat confined."

Ewan Shaw had retired from the Highland Wolves to take up the role of spy master based in London. "How is he aiding your search?"

"Sir Ewan is using his intelligence contacts to pinpoint the locations of French Afflicted. I have a theory that the highest concentration of them will be found around the mage responsible. Unfortunately, so far all the ones we have uncovered are almost equidistant from all the mages." She touched one of the pillars and a face appeared above it. Small eyes squinted from a round face with a long beard.

Hannah suppressed a shudder. What sort of mind had conceived of the evil curse in the first place? Even during a time of war, how did a person justify creating weapons that killed so many innocent people? She wondered if the one who did it might have trouble sleeping at night. Or might even have succumbed to his own creation. "Even if you find the one responsible, how will you persuade him to reveal his original spell?"

Her mother huffed. "I think we will find a way, once we have him pinned down. Moving on to other topics, what do you think of Lord Wycliff after prolonged exposure?"

Hannah snorted and walked to the window seat. She flopped down on the cushion and crossed her arms. "I think he is the most horrid and infuriating man I have ever met. I cannot imagine how he is supposed to help in our work. Is it possible your power was mistaken when it urged you to make him a player on this board?"

With her gloved hand, Seraphina dusted around the edges of the large map. "He is a piece with a purpose—we just can't discern it yet. Have you ever attempted to save an injured animal?"

"Yes." A cat had once become ensnared in a trap set in their garden, meant to catch a stoat eating the chickens.

Next her mother picked up the writing set and dusted underneath. "And what did the creature do, as you worked to save it?"

Hannah remembered that long-ago day. She had been approximately ten years old. "It tried to bite me. What does this have to do with Viscount Wycliff?"

Seraphina stopped dusting and turned a veiled

countenance to her daughter. "An injured animal will lash out, even as you try to free it. In its pain, it cannot distinguish those who hurt it from those trying to help."

"But he is no animal and he should know better. He treats Afflicted women abominably and thinks you should all be rounded up and burned!" How could her mother have any sympathy for the man?

"Ah. So he strikes out from a place of pain and ignorance. How miserable his life must be. Imagine what might happen if someone tried to bring a little light into his darkness."

Hannah scoffed. Let the horrid man wallow in the dark. It seemed the best place for him. "Have you decided on a breed of puppy for me yet?" She'd rather have a loyal dog at her side than the snarling hellhound. Perhaps a lovely spaniel with soft, silky ears.

"Oh, I do believe I know of something that might work."

Though her face was obscured, Hannah couldn't help feeling her mother was smiling beneath her veil.

## 14

Five days later, having made no progress with his inquiries, Wycliff pushed aside the stack of his creditors' invoices and then leaned back in his chair to run a hand through his hair. While he had finally managed to pay off the debts he'd inherited from his father along with the title, in doing so he had ignored his own. Creditors appeared weekly to thrust a new demand for payment into the hands of his elderly retainer.

He kept few staff, requiring only one older couple to see to his needs. The woman cooked and cleaned, the man did everything else. The house was rented, cheap, and in an area bordering on disreputable. He went without a fire in his room so he could save on coal, and simply wore his overcoat inside when the temperature dropped.

His ancestral home in Dorset sat empty, although

he paid a local family to ensure no squatters moved in or removed what furnishings were left.

He was like the Knightleys, selling off everything not nailed down to make ends meet, but the unnatural appetite he had to appease was that of his deceased father. The man had bankrupted the estate to fuel his desires for women and gambling. When Wycliff inherited, society twittered that he would sell the estate, take what residual he could, and scurry away to a dark corner.

Certainly as a young man he had fled the old pile as soon as possible. Only after the war did it become uppermost in his mind. He wanted to put down roots, to belong somewhere, to have a haven that was permanent in a changing world. The estate embodied those things to him and so he fought to keep it. But it was a losing battle.

A manager oversaw the farming of the land and returned sufficient modest profit that after five long years, he had paid off his father's debts. But every year saw the estate fall further into neglect. Essential repairs were deferred. The roof leaked, the windows were draughty, and the wallpaper peeled from the plaster in the front rooms. He wanted to buy new breeding stock of rams and bulls, but there wasn't the money to do so, and no one would extend him credit.

Now he had his own long-neglected creditors to satisfy. While his debts weren't of the magnitude his father's had been, he still felt as though he were swimming through sand. He never made any progress and always fell fractionally behind. Soon he would be sucked under and disappear.

The only way forward was to lay off his staff and give up the small town house. If he took a room in a boarding house, he could slash his expenditures to a minimum and still keep the estate. As a peer, his work for the Ministry of Unnaturals might be sneered upon, but he desperately needed the steady income.

What he needed tonight was a distraction with the few coins he could spare for entertainment. He had heard whispers of a high-stakes bare-knuckle boxing match this evening at his gentleman's club, The Harriers. Some matches attracted crowds of up to twenty thousand spectators, but his club held a private one for members only. He found watching the crowd as diverting as the bouts, as he considered which peers would succumb to blood lust from the safety of their ringside seats.

He was fortunate in that Sir Manly had paid for his annual membership to The Harriers and muttered something about a chap needing some-where for informal meetings with contacts. The club was situated back from Tottenham Court Road and was frequented by those peers not wealthy enough, or entitled enough, to join the more sought-after clubs like White's or Boodle's. The Harriers was removed enough from the wealthier addresses for the members to think they were slumming it, but not so lower class they were at risk of being murdered or robbed.

He took a hired cab to the club, then stood on the footpath and stared up at the squat brick building. It seemed no different than its neighbours. Only the young men walking through its door gave away that it was more than a residence. Inside, one wall of the entrance hall had a large painting of a harrier in flight. Against the other wall ran the counter for the cloakroom. Wycliff passed over his top hat and over-coat to the cheerful-looking young man with auburn hair. He waited for the chit so he could reclaim the items at the end of the evening.

"The ticket?" he finally had to ask. It seemed his lot in life to be plagued by dim-witted people.

The man tapped the side of his head. "No need, sir. My aftermage gift is the ability to know who owns what. I only need to look at you and the right hat and coat will practically jump out at me."

He grunted. The lad was a new addition to the staff. He could see the advantage to his ability; many of the members became drunk and lost their tickets, resulting in a pile of unclaimed clothing at the end of the night.

The imposing doorman opened one side of the double doors to the main hall, where a ring domi-nated the space. Four large posts sat in each corner of a square, and rope was threaded through each. A thin canvas mat covered the square, more to protect the floors from blood and sweat than to offer any protection to falling combatants.

Tables were set up around the edge of the ring. Those who preferred to be close to the action paid extra to be within spitting distance while they wined and dined as men pummelled each other. The crowd of men jostled each other for the best spots to watch. The blacklegs held court at the outer edges, by the walls. They scribbled in their notebooks and gave out odds as coins were placed on one person or another.

A large blackboard listed the evening's boxers. Sixteen men would start the night and through a series of matches, they would be whittled down to the final two, who would fight for the purse at stake. Wycliff headed for the rear of the room, where the floor was raised and a few tables were not yet occupied. When in attendance, he had a usual spot to one side by the wall, where he had a clear line of sight to the action. Then he waved the steward over.

From his corner, he surveyed the crowd. He recognised Lord Talbot at a table close to the ring, surrounded by a handful of his cronies. Wycliff understood the legalities that the Afflicted were dead and that on the cessation of his wife's pulse, the man had become a widower and as such was free to remarry. Yet there was something distasteful about a man who showed such haste in setting aside the woman he had vowed to cherish and protect.

He recalled Miss Hannah Miles's most impassioned defence of the Afflicted and her condemnation of the fickleness of men. She held her father up as a rare example of a man who loved beyond death. On a deep, instinctual level, her words rang true. A man should do anything, including battle death, for the woman who held his heart.

Contrary to what Miss Miles thought of him, he believed himself entirely capable of love. He just hadn't found a female worth bestowing such devotion upon. That surely indicated a fault in the women of society, not in him.

The first bout got underway with a mismatched pair. One man was short of stature and weight and more closely resembled a jockey. The other was taller, heavier, and with a far greater reach. The first few blows broke the smaller man's nose and had blood pouring down his face and chin. Another jab to his temple sent the smaller man reeling over backwards.

Wycliff wondered at the state of a boxer's mind after taking such blows. Did the brain suffer from the walloping? He had seen men killed by blows to the head, or worse, rendered insensible for the rest of their miserable lives. If such a man were to become a donor, did the Afflicted dine on mashed potato rather than sliced cauliflower?

A woman's laugh made him turn his head. An elegant blonde was shown to a table where she could be seen while she watched the matches. Lady Gabriella Ridlington. A *living* woman could not frequent a gentleman's club, to do so risked instant ruin. The Afflicted were different, almost as though their reputations were cast in stone upon death and nothing could do any further damage.

Lady Gabriella would still require to be accompanied by a member of The Harriers. He wondered at her presence. The club didn't seem posh enough for her.

A tall chap bent his head close to hers and from the description Miss Miles had given, he guessed the man to be Mr Jonathon Rowley. Now that he thought about it, he vaguely remembered the man being voted in recently, the fact he could supply the club with champagne at cost being the deciding factor in his favour. This was the perfect opportunity to interview him about the Loburn ball.

He pushed through the crowd to her table and stood at the lady's elbow.

"Lady Gabriella. Any other woman would be ruined if seen here, you must find the lack of a pulse liberating. What brings you to The Harriers—are you a follower of boxing?" Perhaps she hoped someone would dash their brains out on a post so that she could smear them over her toasted bread.

Her eyes were hard behind the porcelain mask as she stared at him. "Lord Wycliff. This is my close friend, Mr Jonathon Rowley. He is disgustingly wealthy, you know, and The Harriers is most fortunate to gain his patronage. I think it such a shame that once great titles and estates should be held in the hands of bankrupt nobles, when men like Mr Rowley could restore them to their former glory."

"If you want to sell that pernicious estate, my lord, I'd be happy to take the weight of responsibility off your threadbare shoulders." Rowley took Lady Gabriella's gloved hand in his and winked at the lady.

Wycliff narrowed his eyes at the other man. They were of equal height, but Rowley had the rounded face that would run to fat later in life. His eyes were shiny and his complexion flushed, as though he had either just run a long distance, or was already exceedingly drunk.

He inhaled and held the scent in his mouth. Something didn't smell right about the man, but he couldn't identify what. The blood of the men being beaten in the ring, the sweat of all the men crammed into the room, and the faint tang of death from Lady Gabriella all combined to make a sharp odour that would make anyone screw up his nose. "What were your movements the night of the Loburn ball? Can anyone account for you?"

Rowley draped an arm over the back of Lady Gabriella's chair and toyed with one of her dangling curls. "I assure you that I was most devoted to the divine Lady G all night."

"And when she danced with other men?" Wycliff picked at the Afflicted woman's account of the evening, looking for a loose thread to unravel. Rowley couldn't have watched her the entire evening.

"Then I watched with jealousy in my breast. With such exquisite beauty before you, how could you look elsewhere?" Rowley's glazed eyes held nothing but devotion for the walking corpse at his side.

How did such a viper inspire such affection? He could only assume Rowley was one of those men who enjoyed being belittled and abused by a domineering woman. "I assume you mean the beauty of her mask? The workmanship is quite exquisite. Given the delicacy of the porcelain, I am amazed that it still manages to hide the rot beneath."

"You are done here, my lord. Go away before you spoil our evening." She waved a hand at him.

A large man pushed through the crowd toward them. The club employed a number of retired pugilists to control its patrons. Even Wycliff knew better than to bait one into a fight.

"This matter is not yet resolved," he said, and then headed back to his table.

As he pushed through the assembled men who screamed at the fighters, a young woman caught his eye. She sat nervously among a group of bucks. The younger men seemed to be ignoring her as they stood and cheered, or jeered, as loudly as everyone else.

There, like a deer surrounded by hounds, was Miss Emma Knightley. What was she doing here? His first instinct was to shepherd the woman out and straight into a hansom cab. Then he remembered she had no pulse. Another Afflicted woman pushing beyond the boundaries that ensured the decency of their living counterparts.

She turned her head and, catching sight of him, quickly looked away.

Most curious. He decided to observe her and watch how events unfolded.

His review of the records of Unwin and Alder showed that Emma Knightley did indeed receive a monthly consignment, and her bill was always paid promptly. And no doubt would continue to be paid until the family ran out of furniture, paintings, and rugs to sell. Her presence with the bucks meant one had vouched for her, like Rowley had for Lady Gabriella. Perhaps she sought a patron to pay for her deliveries.

Lady Gabriella's records showed a curious anomaly. She received not a single delivery, but two every month. What could that mean? Did she succumb to gluttony and consume twice what she needed to sustain her, simply because her wealth allowed it?

She could place a double order for entirely altruistic reasons and might donate the other to a needy Afflicted. But considering what he knew of her nature, that was less likely. Miss Miles's voice in his memory reminded him that the Afflicted could heal damage to their bodies. Did Lady Gabriella conceal some wound in her dead flesh that the excess cauliflower could knit together?

The evening progressed and as boxers were knocked out, the crowd became louder and more raucous. He lost sight of both his quarry among shouting and leaping men. Rather than distracting his mind, the press of so many people made him dwell more on the quiet company of Miss Miles.

She was a woman comfortable with silence. A remarkable trait in a person. He needed to confer with her about what might happen if one of the Afflicted overindulged. Perhaps there was an undead version of gout?

He pulled forth his pocket watch and found it just after two o'clock in the morning. Events in the ring had progressed to the final two bouts, which would decide the men who boxed for the purse. Assuming either managed to stay upright, given their bloody appearances and the way they swayed on their feet.

Wycliff had seen enough. Since he couldn't spot either lady in the crowd, he left the deafening screams in the main hall for the comparative calm of the entrance hall. The cloakroom counter was unattended and the door behind it closed.

He rapped on the desk with his knuckles. "Hello? I require my property."

He couldn't leave without his top hat and overcoat. Finances were far too tight to replace either. Perhaps the man had fallen asleep in the small room beyond. Or more likely, he had gone on a break, thinking no one would leave with the final match about to get under way.

He walked around the counter and tugged on the door handle, only to find it locked. He pulled open the door to the main room and tapped the doorman on the shoulder. He had moved inside to watch the matches.

"Can I help you, my lord?" The man turned his head to Wycliff, but his eyes travelled sideways to watch the bout.

"Yes. I require my hat and coat, but the cloakroom attendant is absent and the door is locked."

A confused look descended over the behemoth's face and, with a resigned sigh, he followed Wycliff back to the hall. At the cloakroom, he reached out and rattled the door handle. "It's locked."

"As I just said." Management hired the men for their imposing bulk, not their mental acuity. "Go fetch a spare key. Then I can reclaim my property."

"Yes, my lord." He strode off with his knuckles practically dragging on the wooden floors.

Wycliff bent to peer at the lock. There was no key on the other side. The man hadn't locked the door and curled up to sleep. He must have wandered away.

As he peered through the keyhole, a faint tang hit his nostrils. A sharp inhale brought more of the rich, metallic odour to his nose. A warning shiver raced over his body.

The muscle reappeared, brandishing a key. He fitted it into the lock and turned it. Wycliff would have bowled the man over to see what was beyond, if his bulk hadn't so completely filled the doorframe.

"Bloody hell!" the man exclaimed, then stumbled backwards.

As he moved out of the way, Wycliff got a glimpse into the room. The cloakroom attendant was indeed taking a nap. A permanent one.

# 15

At nearly three in the morning the household was awakened by the loud banging on the front door. Hannah jerked upright in her bed. The luminous hands on the mantel clock (courtesy of an enchantment by her mother) told her the early hour. Her mind raced ahead of her body. Late night or early morning callers usually meant her father was needed urgently. Before the war, soldiers used to turn up to escort her mother somewhere for the clandestine use of magic, but none sought her abilities since she had passed to the other side.

Hannah grabbed a robe and tied its belt as she hurried down the stairs in the dark. At the bottom, she took a moment to light a lantern while her father's heavier tread followed. She held the light high as her father opened the door.

A man in dark clothing stood on their doorstep. He angled his chin down to keep the light from his eyes. Beyond the porch, drizzle fell. "There's been a murder, sir—an employee of a gentleman's club. You are required most urgently by Viscount Wycliff."

Hannah shared a glance with her father.

*Another one*, she mouthed. For why else would Wycliff be involved?

"Give me ten minutes to dress," Sir Hugh said.

Hannah held up a hand to the man. "*Fifteen* minutes for Sir Hugh and his assistant to dress and to fetch what they require for the examination."

Her father huffed and stared at Hannah. "Very well, fifteen minutes to rouse *my assistant* and collect my things. Off you go, Hannah."

The man rubbed chilled hands together. "The carriage is waiting at the end of the path. Lord Wycliff has secured the scene until you arrive, sir, but please make haste."

Sir Hugh shut the door while Hannah raced up the stairs, one hand on the railing to ensure she didn't miss a step. Upstairs in her bedroom, she tapped a large glass mushroom on her dresser. The object was ensorcelled and awoke on Hannah's command. The mushroom's cap glowed a soft yellow and threw out enough light to dress by.

Next, she grabbed a folded shirt and pair of trousers from a chest. She glanced at the clock as she disrobed and redressed. Ten minutes had ticked by when she pulled on worn boots and tied the laces.

Back down the stairs she hurried, tucking her hair up under a cloth cap as she went. In the parlour they kept her father's bag with an array of instruments he might need if called out at short notice. Hannah had the bag in hand and was waiting as the clock struck the quarter hour.

Sir Hugh's heavy steps reached the bottom of the stairs just as the clock fell silent. "Let us see what awaits us, my boy."

He winked and led the way out the door and down the front path to the waiting conveyance. The driver nodded and they were barely seated when he gave the horses the command to trot on. They journeyed in near dark, the countryside enveloped in an inky blanket. The moon was only a tiny sliver in the sky and up front, the driver relied on the two lanterns on the carriage and the horses' ability to follow the road.

"Another one in less than a week, Papa. What do you think it means?" Hannah whispered the words, even though they were alone, as though she feared that the dark might reply. One nightmare scenario played out in her head—a murderous Afflicted on a feeding frenzy and creating secondary Afflicted in her wake.

Sir Hugh clutched his bag on his knee. "We can only speculate. It could be growing desperation and an out-of-control craving, or perhaps a need to heal damage? It might even be an illegal trade in brains for those Afflicted who cannot afford Unwin and Alder's prices."

"If such were the case, they would be paying footpads to snatch people from darkened streets, not dining on a marquess's footman or an employee of a gentleman's club." She stared out the window and spoke to the starless sky.

The previous crime had been brutal in its execution—the man's head stove in with a paperweight. What would they find when they arrived at their destination tonight? She suspected an equally hasty murder and a missing brain. And Viscount Wycliff stalking the Afflicted in attendance at the event like a fox rounding up chickens.

The carriage drew closer to the bustle of London, heading straight down Oxford Street. Even in the wee hours of the morning there was still activity. Night soil was collected and coal delivered under cover of darkness. Members of the *ton* were still out playing and they would then sleep away the day in a lifestyle perfect for any vampyres among them. Women of the night plied their trade, ignoring the light rain as they hoped to earn sufficient coin to feed themselves and their children.

The carriage turned left into Tottenham Court Road and then stopped about halfway along. The driver opened the door and gestured toward a red brick building that seemed as high as it was wide. "Lord Wycliff awaits you inside, sir."

Hannah glanced around, wondering what sort of establishment he had summoned them to. She stayed close to the bulk of her father as they approached the entry doors. Two enormous men glared at them and she huddled closer to the doctor.

"Sir Hugh Miles," he said to the men guarding the front doors. "Lord Wycliff sent for me."

The men exchanged looks, then one gestured for them to enter and closed the door again behind them. Inside was an entrance hall with a wooden floor and a large painting of a bird on one wall.

"The Harriers," her father said.

For a gentleman's club, the air was permeated with a sharp tang of sweat and blood that made Hannah wrinkle her nose. Double doors to the next room were propped open and they peeped in the doorway. Beyond was a large, mostly empty room. Two men had buckets and mops and were swabbing the floor.

"Whatever went on in here?" she asked her father.

He pointed to the roped-off square covered in blood and spittle. "Bare-knuckle boxing. Quite popular in some circles."

Hannah shuddered. How horrid. Why on earth would men pummel themselves bloody for the entertainment of others?

A door opened to the side of the entrance and the wraith appeared behind them on silent feet.

"This way, Sir Hugh." He glanced at Hannah, then looked again with narrowed eyes.

She tugged the peak of her cap down lower. Usually no one paid any attention to Sir Hugh's assistant and she hoped he wouldn't denounce her in front of the few staff. While society knew that she assisted her father in his laboratory, it would never be considered seemly for a woman to attend a murder scene. Instead, Sir Hugh's assistant attended the more gruesome call-outs.

"My lord," she whispered and clutched her father's bag more tightly.

He grunted. "At least no one will deny you entry to the club for being a woman with a pulse."

She rocked back on her heels. It hardly made a woman's heart race to be told she looked just like a young lad, even if that was the disguise she adopted for the sake of propriety.

With a lift of one corner of his lips, he dismissed Hannah and turned to her father. "Management of The Harriers are cooperating fully. We took an accounting of those present before they were allowed to leave. Although I already know the Afflicted present this evening."

"Noblewomen were here? Surely not." Sir Hugh glanced back to the near deserted room.

"Two were among the crowd. But let us deal with

more pressing matters first." Wycliff's face remained impassive; no emotion flickered across his solemn countenance as he referred to the Afflicted.

They crossed to a counter. The door beyond was closed and Lord Wycliff pulled a key from his pocket. "I ensured the scene would be undisturbed and locked until you arrived."

Her father entered the room first and Hannah followed. The unfortunate victim had met his end in the small cloakroom. His body was collapsed on a coat and his arms outstretched, as though guarding it like a broody hen with chicks. There was even a fox overlooking the scene.

The fox crossed his arms and guarded the door. "Sir Hugh, can you confirm whether this was done by the same culprit?"

"The lights, if you please, Hannah," Sir Hugh said as he contemplated the scene before them.

While her father made a preliminary examination, Hannah opened the large bag and extracted two mirrors on folding stands. She set them up to capture the light from a nearby lantern and then angled the mirrors until a direct beam shone on the man's head.

"Ingenious," Wycliff murmured.

Hannah held out a hand to help her father kneel on the floor. Then she handed him a magnifying glass. Careful not to create a shadow, the doctor examined the edges of the wound.

Hannah took advantage of the silence to survey

the room. Coat hooks lined three walls, and a number of overcoats and cloaks were hung, waiting for their owners. A shelf ran above the hooks and held hats. Stands held umbrellas and canes.

Moving her inspection to the floor, she saw a piece of the man's scalp with auburn hair still intact had been tossed to the corner like the discarded top on a box containing a present. A walking cane with a solid, round brass top lay nearby, having escaped from its stand. The brass orb was discoloured with what at first glance appeared to be rust. Closer inspection revealed the red hairs clinging to the brass end.

"The murderer used the brass-topped cane," Hannah murmured. "Did no one hear him call out?" Two brutal deaths now, and the only screaming had come from the party who had discovered the body. How did these victims remain silent while fatal blows were rained down upon them?

Dark eyes swept over her. "No. The Harriers was exceedingly loud this evening. The men were shouting at the fighters, and you could barely hear yourself think over the din. The Afflicted had locked the door behind herself when she was finished, which further delayed the discovery of the body. We assumed the attendant had taken a break."

Sir Hugh peered at the outer edges of the wound with his magnifying glass, before turning his attention to the interior of the skull. "The brain has been removed, the same as the Loburn footman. The tweezers, please, Hannah—there is something in here that does not belong."

She placed the long-nosed tweezers in his outstretched hand.

Sir Hugh gave the prongs an experimental tap together, then with a steady hand he reached inside the skull. Hannah angled the mirror to shine light where he directed the tweezers. At length he huffed and slowly withdrew them, a tiny, bloody sliver clutched between the pincers.

"What is it?" Wycliff asked, peering at the cream-coloured chip.

Sir Hugh held the magnifying glass over the object as he turned the tweezers in his grasp, to examine it from different angles. "I believe it is a piece of a fingernail. The murderer used their bare hands to scoop out the brain and in their haste, a piece broke off."

Wycliff swore. "Everybody has left already. I did not think to examine their hands."

Hannah reached into her father's bag and found a small glass vial. She removed the stopper and he dropped the broken nail inside. "You had no way of knowing the murderer had left something behind."

Hannah surveyed the pattern made by the blood in the room. "He fought, whereas the footman was either done in or rendered unconscious with the first blow."

"How can you be so sure?" Wycliff turned to her.

Hannah pointed to the blood splatters that covered many of the coats and hats. "The blood trail moves, almost as though he spun around. Perhaps to confront the person who did this?"

"The murderer would have had blood upon their clothing and hands," Sir Hugh said.

Wycliff grunted. "Many people had blood on their clothing this evening, especially those closer to the ring. The area around the fighters looks not unlike this scene."

"There might be a clue in whose coats remain and whose are missing? The murderer might have gone and taken the bloodstains with them." Hannah gestured to the remaining garments on hooks.

Wycliff made a growling noise in the back of his throat. "A possibility we cannot explore, since no tickets are used here. The attendant was new and an aftermage, his gift the ability to know which items belonged to whom."

Sir Hugh turned his attention to the ball end of the cane used. "Yet again our murderer has used what they found at hand. First a paperweight, now a cane."

"But two in one week, Papa. This is most unusual." Hannah stared at the deceased man. He had fought against his demise. Did he perhaps scratch his killer? Hannah peered more closely at the dead man's outstretched hands.

Wycliff tracked her with his black gaze. "Why is the frequency unusual? Are these creatures not driven by a monstrous appetite?"

Hannah swallowed a breath and took a moment to steel herself before responding. Her instinct was to snap back, but his question was not unreasonable. "The hunger is the body's way of directing the Afflicted to what it needs to ward off the rot. But it is an appetite that is sated with a small amount of matter. This is gluttonous behaviour."

Her father huffed. They had made extensive studies to find the lowest amount needed to sustain one of the unfortunate women. "One Afflicted requires one brain per month. A sliver a day keeps the rot away," Sir Hugh said.

Wycliff arched a dark eyebrow at her father. Not everyone shared her father's morbid sense of humour.

"A frugal Afflicted can make one brain last for six weeks without any ill effects. Beyond that, death seeks to claim their forms. But what we see here is an indulgence of excess for no apparent reason. To do this would not be worth their exposure, for their own continued safety." Hannah faltered, unable to find the words to understand why one of the Afflicted would commit such a crime. If they exercised moderation, they would have no need to seek nourishment from other sources. Instead of voicing the ideas swirling in her head, she instead contemplated her hands. From which finger had the murderer lost the nail?

"There is one more possibility, Hannah. The Afflicted may be seeking to heal a wound. That might explain the frenzied attack." Sir Hugh moved from his cramped spot on the floor and stood.

Wycliff grunted. "The attendant was an after-mage, and, I have discovered, so was Dunn, the Loburn footman. Do you think that is relevant?"

"Perhaps this Afflicted has discovered something we have not, Papa?" Hannah bit her lower lip as she tried to think through the consequences.

*Hypothesise, then strategise.* They had not yet studied the effect the type of brain might have, and she was grasping to find some sort of reason or logic in such a senseless crime. A wound of some signifi-cance seemed the most likely cause, especially if the lady could not afford the additional purchases from Unwin and Alder.

Her father let out a sigh and dropped the magni-fying glass back into his bag. "We won't know until we commence our study. I have some early notes about excess, from when your mother and her friends were first Afflicted and we were learning. As you can imagine, the war gave us a plentiful supply of brains no longer in use."

"Who did you see among the revellers?" Hannah asked Wycliff, curious as to whether he had narrowed down his suspect list.

"Lady Gabriella Ridlington was here with her companion Mr Rowley, and Miss Emma Knightley with a party of friends."

Hannah stared at him, but in her mind's eye, she saw Emma crying over a stain on her gown.

# 16

The next day, Wycliff was summoned to the Ministry of Unnaturals by his superior. He arrived at their offices in Whitehall to find a vacant front desk. The fledgling ministry was still in the process of hiring staff and had yet to find a secretary.

Wycliff considered requesting an office in the small, squat building. If he set up a camp bed, he could further reduce his expenditures by sleeping in his office. With nothing else to fill his days, he would be wedded to the job anyway.

He walked down the hall and rapped on a dark wood door.

"Enter," a voice said from beyond.

Within the office, he found General Sir Manly Powers and Sir Hugh Miles deep in conversation.

"Ah, Wycliff, take a seat. Sir Hugh has some

information he wishes to impart." Sir Manly gestured to a vacant sofa before the fireplace.

"What of Miss Miles? Will she be joining us?" He cast around the room, but she didn't appear to be hiding behind Sir Manly's desk. He looked forward to provoking a passionate response from her in the defence of the undead like her mother.

Sir Hugh sat adjacent to Wycliff. The large man leaned forward, arms on thighs, and clasped his beefy hands together. "No. There are things about the Afflicted that Lady Miles and I do not think appropriate for Hannah to hear. Nor is it relevant to the research she undertakes. What I am about to impart to you must be kept confidential."

"Very well. You have my full attention." Wycliff had feared the girl might hamper his investigation and here was confirmation—there was pivotal knowledge she lacked. He rested one arm along the back of the sofa as he waited for the surgeon to begin.

"In the summer of 1813, Seraphina and two of her friends—ordinary ladies, not mages—were poisoned by a French agent. It was a cowardly assassination to prevent England's most powerful mage from helping us to victory. All three women became violently ill almost immediately and within hours, slipped into unconsciousness. Despite my medical knowledge, I found myself powerless and no remedy made any difference to their conditions. Three days later, I held my wife in my arms as her heart stopped beating and she departed this world." He choked over the words, as though reliving the experience.

*A man who loved beyond death*, Miss Miles whispered in Wycliff's ear. He waved a hand to dismiss the phantom. "How long did Lady Miles remain that way?"

Sir Hugh unclasped his hands and stared at his palms. "Two days. I refused to allow anyone to remove her. I was not yet ready to say a final farewell to my heart's companion. You can only imagine my joy when she sat up and said she felt...*odd*. Only upon a thorough examination did I discover she had returned to consciousness, but not to life."

Information was intelligence, and Wycliff hoped that somewhere in the narration about the origins of the Afflicted were clues that would enable him to identify the murderer. "And so she became the first Afflicted. What of the other two women?"

"One had already been buried and she was hastily dug up. The experience of being entombed in a coffin permanently affected Mrs Edgar's mind. She was hysterical when freed and her erratic fits never subsided. Lady Tennent fared somewhat better, as she still awaited burial. Her husband was alerted to her condition when she banged on the nailed coffin lid. Poor chap nearly had a heart attack."

Sir Manly chortled to himself and his enormous curled moustache wagged up and down. "Colonel

Tennent was always susceptible to frights. Never thought he should have been put in the field."

Wycliff wanted the facts, not the embellished version more suited to a work of fiction. "Did the women immediately crave brains?"

Sir Hugh leaned forward and poured a glass of water from the decanter on the low table before them. "No. All three women were put under my care because they all felt ill and, of course, had no pulse. My superiors wanted answers, but I was fumbling in the dark to determine what had happened and how to remedy it. The French had an agent posing as a maid to poison a pot of tea, but the woman took her own life before we could question her further."

"Your wife must have supplied some thoughts from her unique perspective?" There must be some advantage to having an undead mage working for England. She had already mentioned how her magical ability had *transformed* when her pulse stopped. Since she dwelt with the undead, did she look through the veil she wore from the valley of death? He had stared death in the face and even from this side, the experience had altered him.

"Seraphina said the poison was tainted with the dark arts and that she could taste it as it stole her life. Over the last three years, we have concluded it was a merging of science and black magic. Neither would have worked in isolation. That is why we work together to try to undo what has been done." Sir Hugh sipped the water.

How did a person recognise they needed to consume human brains? The very idea was anathema and made him shudder. Vampyres, with their need to drink human blood, didn't seem as obscene; he imagined one sipping what appeared to be red wine from a goblet. He couldn't think of a culinary equivalent for an Afflicted except for sitting down to a meal of tripe and onions, even if Unwin and Alder labelled their product pickled cauliflower.

"When did their appetites emerge?" he asked.

Blunt fingernails tapped the side of the tumbler in Sir Hugh's hand. "Over a period of weeks we tried a number of recipes, but the women could not stomach even the lightest broth and their bodies rejected the nourishment. Their hunger grew, but we could find nothing in the kitchens to satisfy them."

"Not many kitchens stock brains," Sir Manly pointed out.

"Did they deteriorate without sustenance?" The Afflicted needed to consume on a regular basis to keep the rot at bay. He had augmented his knowledge of the Afflicted thanks to his conversations with Miss Miles.

"Yes. After three weeks, I noticed the discolouration in the extremities. Their complexions took on the grey, dull appearance of the dead. They smelt of the decay nibbling at their bodies. Soldiers pressed cloths to their own faces as the odour grew and spread from our tent. Whispers grew, calling the women *undead*, for while they had no pulse they walked among us. I began referring to them as the Afflicted, to alleviate some of the men's fears. The general thought it made their condition sound more medical than ungodly."

Wycliff agreed with the common soldiers—they were ungodly. A few believed it so vehemently that they had taken to protesting outside Parliament, demanding the undead be expunged from the earth. A position that wasn't well received when those women were closely allied to men in power. "Did all three women exhibit the same symptoms?"

"In Lady Tennent and Mrs Edgar, the rot ate their fingers, toes, and noses first. In Seraphina, it advanced up her legs at an accelerated rate. Possibly it affected her differently, since she is a mage and the others ordinary. As the flesh and muscles of her lower legs turned putrid, she begged me to remove the limbs." Sir Hugh halted his narrative and rose from his seat. He paced for a moment or two in front of the fireplace. Then he stopped and stared at the fire burning in the grate, one hand curled on the mantel. "I was a damned fine field surgeon. I have lost count of how many amputations I have performed and of the lives I have saved. But it is another thing entirely to remove your wife's limbs. She steadied my hand upon the saw when I would have faltered."

"Not an easy thing when your wife is the patient, old chap. But I think the viscount here is keen to hear how you discovered what the women needed to keep them going, and how that might affect his investigation." Sir Manly's tone was solemn but bracing as he prodded his contemporary.

"Of course." Sir Hugh let go of the mantel. "It was while I removed her legs that there was an incident close to camp. Our soldiers fought a decisive but messy skirmish with the enemy. I was focused on concluding the double amputation on Seraphina, and failed to notice that Mrs Edgar had escaped her captivity."

"The battle drew her." It took no effort for Wycliff to conjure the scene in his mind. Death had a particular stench that was hard to escape. Did the Afflicted have better noses when dead, or did their ravenous state enhance their senses?

Sir Hugh nodded. "Quite. I believe the odour attracted her. We have all seen battles—the bodies scattered with a variety of injuries. There are often blows or shots to the head and the brains of soldiers spilled over the ground. She fell upon the remains to satisfy her unnatural hunger. That was when Lady Tennent joined her friend. The odour had likewise drawn her away from camp and she, too, fell on the dead soldiers."

War does strange things to men. Some become inured to violence, while a few are driven mad by it.

While Wycliff could easily summon the memory of a battlefield strewn with fallen men, his mind shied away from imagining the desecration those women had committed. "I assume the women were discovered?"

"A group of British soldiers found them. The two of them were cracking open the skulls of the dead with rocks and shovelling handfuls of brains into their mouths." The surgeon beat a rhythm on the mantel with his short nails, like the thrum of men marching in time.

Wycliff swallowed the bile that rose in his throat. "Even in the aftermath of a battle, that would have been a disgusting sight."

The drumbeat fell silent and Sir Hugh's hand dropped to his side. "The soldiers were enraged to find the women eating their fallen comrades. They opened fire. Bullets riddled their bodies, but they couldn't stop feeding."

How do you kill something that is already dead? "Did the soldiers cease firing when they realised bullets were ineffective?"

"Yes. So they switched to their swords." Sir Hugh returned to the low table for his glass of water as silence dropped over the room.

There was no need for him to expand. Wycliff could fill in the blanks. He had seen men in the throes of battle rage and he suspected that little had remained of the two women once the soldiers had vented their anger. There was one point that itched in his mind, though. Bullets hadn't stopped the women as no heart beat in their chests. Surely swords would also be ineffective? "Did swords halt their feeding frenzy?"

Sir Hugh blew out a deep breath. "Despite my studies over the last few years, I am no closer to discovering what keeps the Afflicted animated apart from saying *it's magic*. We have learned that injuries that would be fatal to an ordinary person are but an inconvenience to them. Despite hacking their bodies in pieces, the women still sought to feed. Severed fingers reached for brain matter in the grass to carry like ants to lips that opened and closed, waiting to be fed. Feet shuffled to other pieces. The soldiers built a bonfire and let the flames consume what was left of Mrs Edgar and Lady Tennent."

"And that was how you learned what they craved and that only fire can put an end to an Afflicted." Which knowledge had led to Messieurs Unwin and Alder becoming wealthy purveyors of human brains. Many palms had been liberally greased with coin to keep that information out of the newspapers. It was something of an open secret. People knew, but didn't want to know at the same time. The less attention it drew, the easier it was to pretend it didn't happen. Until one of the Afflicted started dining on the servants. "As informative as this has been, how is it relevant to my current investigation?"

Sir Manly twisted one end of his fancifully curled moustache. "Murder requires a motive, Wycliff. You have been focused on an Afflicted satisfying a hunger. Sir Hugh is expanding your knowledge of potential motives."

The large surgeon laced his fingers together. "When I had finished amputating Seraphina's legs, she urged me to go investigate. She said the smell was making her stomach grumble and was most compelling and, at long last, she thought it might be something she could eat. I found the soldiers disposing of her companions. From what I saw, even in their dismembered state, the wounds were beginning to heal. If they had not been burned, I believe the women would have pieced themselves back together. The craving is the body's way of signalling what they needed in order to heal."

The French had it within their power to create an army that could never be stopped. Soldiers who would keep on fighting even when dismembered. Yet they had used that power to contaminate face powder instead. No wonder they'd lost the war.

Wycliff thought through the implications. "The Afflicted murderer could be seeking to heal a wound. You did suggest that last night."

"It would need to be a wound large enough that the Afflicted's usual ration is insufficient. On the Peninsula, I took a brain back to our tent and mixed it with oats. I fed it to Seraphina and told her it was something the men were cooking outside. As she consumed the gruel, the amputation wounds healed completely. It did not reverse the older rot, though. An excess can heal recent wounds, but not anything older than a few weeks."

"An injury, then, that is perhaps less than a month old and serious enough to require two fresh brains, but located somewhere that it could be concealed to escape notice in company." Or had the murderer consumed more? Wycliff had enquired of the Runners and magistrates for information about murders in London over the last month that might be similar.

"Yes, given the level of feeding, I would say a rather large and nasty wound. I'm not sure how they could hide it and still attend the Loburn ball." Sir Hugh unclasped his hands to wave them in the air several inches apart, as though imagining the size of such an injury.

This was information Wycliff could use. The murderer would seek to conceal such an injury, but there might be signs in the way they carried or conducted themselves. "If they have now healed, they will be impossible to find."

"Unless there is another murder," Sir Hugh said. "Or another motive."

Wycliff narrowed his eyes at the former field surgeon. "Another motive? What are you not telling me?"

"One of the soldiers later remarked upon the scene on the battlefield. The women were making moaning noises as they ate. He likened it to the sounds of pleasure his wife made during the marital act." Sir Hugh's bushy eyebrows rose up and down.

Wycliff's eyebrows shot up in silent conversation with Sir Hugh's. "They found pleasure in the act of consumption?"

"Most of the Afflicted I have studied report a sense of enjoyment or fulfilment upon consuming their daily sliver. A feeling such as you or I might experience when savouring a fine brandy at the end of the day. The two unfortunate companions of Seraphina are the only examples we have of such wanton excess. Given that they had gone weeks without any sustenance, I cannot say if their frenzy was the result of trying to heal or if they were driven by pleasure. I'm sure you can extrapolate the heightened sensation an Afflicted may find in gluttony."

Now he understood why they had kept such knowledge from Miss Miles. Hardly an appropriate discussion to have with a maiden who would not understand the type of bliss derived. He had thought he hunted a murderer who sought to sate an appetite. He might still be right—he just had the wrong type of appetite. "Could an Afflicted become addicted to large feedings, such as a person who takes laudanum regularly?"

Sir Hugh refilled his glass from the pitcher on the

low table. "The majority of the Afflicted are able to control their habit, as might most of us with alcohol or laudanum. But just as some men become opium addicts or drunkards, there is a deficit of character that makes a very few of the Afflicted unable to control their appetite."

What danger to society did the Afflicted women represent? "At the Loburn ball you told me of similar murders committed two years ago. What happened to those who could not control their hunger?"

Sir Manly and Sir Hugh exchanged a long glance.

"We have a location where they are interred, so as not to be a danger to the general population," Sir Manly answered. "After the murders, we quickly identified and removed those Afflicted who could not control themselves and who presented a danger to others."

Wycliff stored the information away. He might have been looking at the problem from the wrong angle. Instead of looking for an Afflicted behind in their bill, he might need to look for any with recent injuries or one who exhibited a tendency to addiction when alive. Or perhaps, one who had escaped this carefully undisclosed location. "Could one have escaped and continued their murder spree?"

"No. Lady Miles erected wards around the property and there is a constant guard. No one goes in or out without our knowledge," Sir Manly said.

Then someone had escaped their net two years ago. But how had they gone undetected for so long? "I asked Miss Miles if there was any difference to an Afflicted whether they consumed the brain of an aftermage or an ordinary individual. She did not know, but is this also intelligence you have withheld from her?"

Sir Hugh huffed. "No. I keep very little from Hannah. That is not a line of enquiry we have thought to pursue. On the Peninsula, we simply didn't have the records or the time to verify the origins of the donors I used to keep Seraphina in a stable condition. It is a possibility. You would also need to factor in that the murderer is consuming these minds fresh, whereas what Unwin and Alder supply is pickled."

"Both victims were aftermages," Wycliff told them. "The Loburn footman was seventh generation, his ability described by his fellow servants as a vague tingling when someone upstairs required him. The cloakroom attendant possessed fifth-generation magic." There were so many strands to this tangled web. Which ones were relevant and would lead him to the killer?

Sir Hugh frowned as he considered the possibility. "If there is indeed a difference in the type of mind consumed, then it is possible our murderer may have developed a taste for magic."

Wycliff tugged at the thread, testing whether it

would unravel or entangle him further. "And following that line, they may want to dine on something more powerful next time. How many third-generation aftermages are there in London?"

Sir Manly blew out a breath that made the waxed ends of his moustache quiver. "Too many to watch them all."

At least Miss Miles wouldn't be a target. The children of mages were as ordinary and powerless as those without a mage ancestor.

*No,* a voice whispered from the depths of his mind. *She isn't ordinary. Far from it.*

## 17

Wycliff walked down the wide stairs to the street with slow steps as he gathered his thoughts. The conversation with Sir Hugh Miles had been enlightening and had given him a new avenue to consider. The Afflicted murderer he sought could be seeking to heal a large wound, or more likely, they might have succumbed to a type of addiction and were gorging themselves on human minds in pursuit of pleasure.

His afternoon spent at Unwin and Alder comparing client records to the list from the Loburn ball had revealed that six Afflicted had been present that night. Of them, only two had been present at The Harriers. Unless the Afflicted he sought didn't use Unwin and Alder. That was a slim possibility, but one he would have to consider. Otherwise, he had only two suspects, neither of whom appeared to exhibit signs of substantial injury, nor did they appear to have the disheveled outward appearance of addicts.

Wycliff dismissed Mr Jonathon Rowley; despite his attachment to Lady Gabriella, he couldn't see how the man could be involved. What man would be a party to such ungodly appetites? How could any man kiss a mouth that had licked clean a still warm skull? While Lady Gabriella had a reputation for excess, that was more than met by the size of her father's fortune. The woman already consumed two brains a month. Was that insufficient to curb her appetites?

The late Lady Albright hovered near the bottom of his very short list. A heavily veiled woman had been seen outside The Harriers, but that wasn't enough to assume it was she. It might not even have been one of the Afflicted, but a woman veiled for some other reason, such as a recent bereavement, or an unwillingness to let her identity be known at a boxing match.

However, his review of Unwin and Alder's records showed that Lady Albright received one delivery every six weeks—a regime that would leave her on the sharp edge of hunger. It wasn't a big jump to imagine her supplementing her meagre diet. Except that ran contrary to the fresh intelligence he had obtained from Sir Hugh. Instinct whispered that mere hunger alone wasn't a sufficient motive.

He couldn't completely remove the lady's name as a suspect. Her husband had been present, jeering and drinking at a table up at the front. Who knew—the unfortunate woman might have followed her husband there to talk, but made it no farther than the cloakroom. All of society knew there was bad blood between them.

There was something distasteful in how Albright paraded his much younger wife and her fecundity for all to see. He had even been heard to advise men in unsatisfactory marriages to follow his example and seek out a jar of infected face powder to give to their inconvenient wives.

Wycliff made a mental note to pay a visit to the late Lady Albright and pick at her biggest wound—her husband. No woman could be as patient and understanding as Miss Miles painted her to be. He was sure that beneath the surface he would find simmering resentment ready to burst forth in a fit of murderous rage.

As luck would have it, as he plowed southwest along the pavement with pedestrians jumping out of his way, he spied Miss Knightley on the street. She was accompanied by her mother and a bored-looking maid carrying an armload of parcels. All three were dressed in varying shades of brown and looked like three country mice in town for the day.

Wycliff changed course to intercept them and planted himself in their way. He became an immovable obstacle they could not avoid. The small party halted and darted looks around him.

"Miss Knightley, I have a quick request. I require you to hold out your hands."

The young woman curled her gloved hands closer to her body and looked to her mother, who hovered at her side. No breath quickened in her chest and she dropped the pretence of inhaling and exhaling.

Did she conceal an injury under her clothing, or had two fresh brains in the last week healed her? Miss Miles had remarked on the lack of rot evident in Miss Knightley. Perhaps she kept the rot at bay by dining on servants descended from mages. Finding her own source of brains would save her parents from selling more furniture to pay Unwin and Alder.

"Just do as he asks, Emma, so that he will go away," Mrs Knightley whispered.

Most would not have heard her, but Wycliff's ears easily snatched the words on the light breeze.

Miss Knightley pushed the strings of her reticule further up her arm and held out her hands, palms up. She was wearing beige gloves made of a soft hide.

Wycliff rolled his eyes. Did she honestly think he wanted to examine her gloves? "You must remove your gloves."

They blocked the flow of pedestrians and created a fork, with people choosing one side or the other to go around them. The curious cast sharp glances at them, disapproval for the inconvenience to others scored into their brows. Wycliff ignored them. He did not care one whit if he inconvenienced the whole of London.

Miss Knightley tugged on the fingertips and stripped off the gloves, which she then handed to her mother. She held out her hands, palms up.

Wycliff inhaled deeply through his nostrils and caught the faint mustiness from the young woman. Dim-witted women were sent to test him. He held a tight rein on his temper. "Turn them over. I wish to see your nails."

She rotated her hands, holding them before her like a child being inspected for cleanliness before she could have dinner. All her nails were filed exceptionally short. Two looked as though they had ripped down into the nail bed and the rest trimmed to match. Her fingertips had the slight blue-grey discolouration that gave away the onset of rot within her body. "You have very short nails. Did you break one recently?"

He wanted to ask, *Perhaps while scooping out a poor man's brain?* But for some reason, he imagined Miss Miles standing by Miss Knightley, shaking her head and reprimanding him for his abrupt questions.

Miss Knightley lifted her fingers and peered at them. "I am often in our garden. Weeding is very rough on the hands."

"Were you not wearing gloves?" He had difficulty imagining one of the Afflicted on her knees gardening. Was there even a need to wear gloves if they could heal wounds to their flesh? Any scrapes or scratches would be gone before they walked inside. Especially if they were well fed.

"Sometimes I forget." She snatched her gloves back from her mother and shoved her hands into the leather.

"Do nails grow back as easily as your flesh heals itself?" If one decided to cut off all their hair, would they awake the next morning to find it had all grown back?

Miss Knightley smoothed the leather down each finger. "Yes. So long as we continue to feed regularly both hair and nails continued to grow as they have always done. Is that all?"

Now that he had her captive, there was one more question. "No. What were you doing at The Harriers last night? Do you often watch bare-knuckle boxing?"

Mrs Knightley let out a startled yelp and one hand clutched at her throat. The woman was rather highly strung and reminded him of a whippet they'd had when he was a child. The dog hadn't lasted long —it took fright at a loud noise one day and dashed out in front of a carriage.

"That is none of your business." For the first time in their short acquaintance, the young woman bit out the words tersely. It appeared that Wycliff had worn away her good manners. Things might get interesting if she succumbed to the same passionate outbursts as Miss Miles occasionally displayed.

Mrs Knightley made gasping noises and now resembled not the whippet, but a fish scooped onto land. "You are mistaken. Emma was at the theatre with respectable ladies last night."

Wycliff ignored the older woman. It was none of his business if the daughter had deceived her mother about her activities. "Your whereabouts is my business when an Unnatural commits a murder during an event you attended."

Miss Knightley glanced at her mother, then her gaze dropped and focused on the toes of her boots. "A gentleman took me. He thought it might be diverting. I did not find it particularly entertaining and so I left early. Now we really must be on our way."

She looped her arm through her mother's and half dragged the older woman along the pavement.

He watched them be swallowed up by the other pedestrians and then stepped to the curb and hailed a hansom cab. His luck held out at the Ridlington residence. The lady in question was in the foyer, about to leave.

"Oh. You," she muttered as he crossed the threshold. "I had hoped never to see you again. Where is your dreary little mouse today—hiding in the wainscoting?"

He might be rude, abrupt, and intolerant of

stupidity, but he would never be unnecessarily cruel for his own entertainment. Lady Gabriella was the type who made a sport of baiting others. He much preferred Miss Miles's quiet presence to the empty nattering of other women. At least when she spoke, she was usually worth listening to.

"Miss Miles has important work to do assisting her father." He wondered if they had made a start on the new study and what, as time unfolded, they would learn about the different feeding habits of the Afflicted.

The lady laughed, the sound constrained by the edge of porcelain around her lips. "Work. Of course her type works. It's not as though eligible men would ever line up outside her door. Poor thing is too unattractive to ever make coin on her back, so she will need some activity to keep her when her parents are gone."

If no young bucks had noticed Miss Miles, then perhaps that was their loss. There were many ways an intelligent woman could make her way in the world without resorting to selling her body. At least Miss Miles was capable of interesting discourse once her mind was activated, whereas Lady Gabriella would always be a hollow echo. For once, Wycliff kept that thought inside his head. "I wish to inspect your fingernails, Lady Gabriella."

She waved to the man at her side while she

fiddled with the angle of her hat. "Show him, Jonathon, so that we might be on our way."

Her constant companion stepped forward. His complexion was flushed as though he were developing a fever, and tiny droplets of sweat clung to his brow. He swiped a handkerchief over his forehead and returned it to his pocket before holding out his hands. All ten nails were chewed to the quick. He flashed a quick grin. "I'm a nail biter. Terrible habit, I know. Developed it when Father made me work in the brewery. Long nails would get ripped clean off."

Wycliff grunted deep in his throat. Damn. Not that he thought the wastrel would have any involvement. He was too busy throwing around his surplus money. He dismissed the man. "I need to see *your* hands, Lady Gabriella, not those of Mr Rowley."

"I don't remove my gloves for anyone."

"You will for me." Why did peers think they were above the law? Just because Death had failed to snatch her, didn't mean Wycliff would also fail. He puzzled over her Unwin and Alder account. Two pickled cauliflower a month. One in plain vinegar, one spiced to her own recipe. Did she seek to heal a wound, but found the preserved matter insufficient?

She stared at him, her eyes hard behind the delicate mask. The painted blush to her cheeks belied the resistance oozing from her person. No, she would eat more than she required for the same reason she drank champagne instead of water—because she could.

"If it will get rid of you." She pulled off the gloves and passed them to Rowley.

Wycliff leaned forward to inspect her hands and bit back his disgust. Rot nibbled at the ends. Many of the nails were missing where they had sloughed off her decomposing flesh. The sharp odour stabbed up into his nostrils and he squeezed them shut to stop the unwanted invasion.

"Satisfied?" She snatched back her gloves and presented her back as she put them on again.

"For now." He was no further ahead. Both his main suspects lacked fingernails, and for plausible explanations.

"Don't return, Viscount Wycliff. I intend to let my father know that you have made a nuisance of yourself. It will be another black mark against your name."

He huffed in sardonic amusement. What more could society to do him? "I have collected so many such black marks that I imagine my name is fully coloured in by now."

He walked back to the main road and considered his next course of action. He planned to dig around the fourth name on his list—the late Lady Albright. No one could be as forgiving as her reputation painted her to be. There must be lingering resentment. Perhaps she sought an excess of brains to cure her rot and restart her heart.

None of the women looked as though they harboured serious injury, nor did they have the glazed or desperate look that came from being in the grip of addiction. It was possible he had overlooked something or someone. Once he had questioned the late Lady Albright, he would re-examine all he had learned so far.

He returned to the modest terrace house and was admitted by the maid. The lady in question and her cousin were seated at a table, playing cards.

Mrs Hamilton threw her hand of cards to the green felt when she caught sight of him. "I must talk to the housekeeper." She nodded at him as she passed.

The black-veiled creature didn't move from the table, the playing cards still clutched in her gloved hands.

"There was another murder. At The Harriers club, last night." Wycliff clasped his hands behind his back. Was he speaking to a rational being or a veil-draped mannequin?

"It was not I." Lady Albright placed her cards on the top of the pack.

"Your husband was present." He wasn't sure what he sought here. But instinct told him that if he needled the right spot, he would learn something.

Her hand curled around the pack of cards. "But I

didn't go in. I only walked as far as the entrance and then realised I was being foolish and left."

That was unexpected, and easier than he anticipated. The lady had just confessed she had been present and within sight of where the attendant had been murdered.

"Is it your custom to stalk your former husband in the evenings?"

She let go of the deck and curled her hand into a fist. "He is my husband before God. The law might declare him a widower, but I am not buried. I might lack a heartbeat, but I still have feelings. He cast me aside after all the loyal years I gave him."

"Does that make you angry?" he murmured. He would have thought her anger would be directed at the man in question, not the servants around him. Or were her actions meant as a warning to her husband, a message that he was next?

She removed her hands from the table and curled them into her lap. "No, I am disappointed. I only seek to talk to him, but I am dead and *persona non grata* to him. I may reside in Hell, Lord Wycliff, but I am no murderer."

He would be the judge of that. "I wish to see your fingernails."

She pulled off the gloves and laid her hands flat on the table.

Wycliff took a step back. Most of the nails were entirely absent, the fingers rotted well down to the knuckle. Decay spread over her wrists and disappeared up under the long sleeves of her afternoon dress.

"I was one of the last to access the 'pickled cauliflower,' and so the curse devoured more of me than any of the others," she said, her head bowed over her rotting flesh.

For the first time, Wycliff felt something stir within him, provoked either by the sight of the curse eating the woman, or her forlorn tone. "I am sorry," he managed to say.

Looking at fingernails wasn't helping. It was time to have a chat with Lord Albright and see if the man lived in fear of his skull's being cracked open.

## 18

Hannah sat in the window seat of the library. She had removed her shoes and sat cross-legged with a large ledger open before her. The book was ensorcelled so that entries made in its twin kept by Unwin and Alder would appear on the pages of the volume held by Hannah.

Sir Manly Powers had granted them permission to study the effects, if any, of the type of sustenance the Afflicted consumed. When she visited the premises of Unwin and Alder, she had been met with a most enthusiastic response. The owners were delighted to fully cooperate in the study.

New procedures were set in motion at the resurrectionists' and her mother had worked an enchantment on the ledgers. Employees at Unwin and Alder recorded the details of each donor—name, date of birth, gender, and date of donation. Each entry was then assigned a number, which would be used to identify and track whose brains were delivered to whom.

Seated at the library desk, Seraphina studied the enormous tome that contained the mage genealogies. Each double-page spread recorded a mage's seven generations, the names appearing with each birth until the magic trace was exhausted. The mage was counted as generation one. The second generation were devoid of magic, like Hannah. While she could feel magic, she had no ability of her own. The third generation were the most powerful aftermages. Generations four through seven possessed an ever more diluted form of magical ability. Some seventh-generation aftermages could only tell if it was going to rain or someone was about to knock on the door.

Hannah called out each name from her ledger and her mother scoured the genealogies to see if the person appeared. If so, Hannah wrote down *A*, for aftermage, and then a number to correspond to their generation.

For the two hours they had laboured, they had very few *A*s to show for their work and the column was filling up with *O*s, for ordinary.

"We may struggle to conduct a viable study, there are so few aftermages among the donors." Hannah called the next name, a Stephen Connors who had died aged twenty-four. As she read each name, she wondered at the life they had led. Who had they loved and what made them laugh?

Seraphina ran a gloved hand over a row of names, searching for *Stephen Connors*. "For all our magical abilities, mages are particularly inept at reproducing. Did you know that during medieval times, it was decreed that all mages had a duty to produce as many children as possible? Those kings wanted to swell their armies with powerful third-generation after-mage troops to defeat their enemies, so they ensured that each mage had a harem of women to impregnate." Pages were flicked over and scanned before she announced, "There's no Stephen Connors here."

Hannah marked an O in the column for Type next to the man's name. "That was rather foolish of those kings. Just as many girls are born as boys. You cannot decide the gender of your child."

Seraphina turned over a few pages. "Ah. A woman with power—*there* is something to give men nightmares. The Middle Ages were our dark times, and a sad chapter in the history of womankind. Female aftermages were considered ungodly, and many a child was smothered at birth. A girl was no safer once she grew to womanhood, as many of our sisters were burned at the stake as witches."

Hannah placed the pen down on a tray and pulled her knees to her chest. "Why did they fear us so?"

"Because they cannot control us. Only weak men

fear strong women. Even female mages were not exempt from the orders of kings." Her mother flicked pages back to near the beginning of the genealogy. Many pages were practically blank, with only a single name inscribed at the top.

"No," Hannah gasped. There were only ever a dozen mages at any one time in all of England, Scotland, and Wales. Each one was valued for their skills, regardless of their gender. "But you are the first female mage in over five hundred years."

More pages were turned until Seraphina stopped at one in particular. "No, I am not. Sadly I am merely the first in five hundred years to live to maturity. Those archaic men of God thought a girl must have stolen a mage's power, and that if they smothered her, the power would be reborn in the rightful male body. Only one female mage escaped those dark days, aided by a mage who gave his life to protect her and the Unnatural creature men sent to kill her."

A wistful smile touched Hannah's lips. She loved that story with its fairy-tale elements. From death and tragedy had arisen a love so strong that the mage had been able to defy man and nature, and gave her lover the only known magically gifted second-generation children—three girls known as the Crows.

"I am glad we live in more enlightened times." A vision of Viscount Wycliff's angry face appeared in the thick glass beside Hannah. To give him his due, while he might not be enlightened, as least he disapproved of men and women equally.

"Even when monarchies and governments stay out of our private business, we still bear very few children. As though magic knows how to restrain itself. She cannot be compelled to create too many of us."

Hannah crept over to her mother and peered over her shoulder. The page she lingered over had the name Seraphina Elizabeth Winyard inscribed at the top. A line connected her name to that of Sir Hugh Joseph Miles and the year 1790—the year they married. A short downward stroke ended in the name Hannah Elspeth Miles and the year 1794.

Her mother rested a finger under her name and the two dates in brackets: 1770–1813.

The year she died.

Her mother's page in the genealogy was destined to remain empty space.

A soft knock came at the library door and then it was pushed open by Mary. She held out a hand toward Hannah. "Letter for you, miss."

"Thank you." Hannah took the slim envelope. When Lizzie wrote to her, the envelopes were normally much fatter as she detailed all the London gossip that had happened that week. She unfolded the single sheet to find a solitary line:

· · ·

*Y*OUR *ASSISTANCE IS NO LONGER REQUIRED.*
*Wycliff*

"I HAVE BEEN DISMISSED. Horrid man—he is convinced Miss Emma Knightley is the murderer." She tossed the letter to the desk.

Her mother took the discarded letter and read the scant missive. "Viscount Wycliff might be unpleasant, but I did not think him unreasonable. He must surely have a reason for suspecting the young woman?"

Hannah bit back her retort. He did have a reason, but that didn't mean she had to agree with him. He was wrong and she would prove him so, if only she could figure out who had committed the crimes.

Seraphina reached out and took Hannah's hand. "You are always seeing the best in people, Hannah, and the viscount sees the worst. What a shame you could not meet somewhere in the middle and share your views."

Hannah frowned at her mother. She didn't want anything to do with the man. By dismissing her, he had removed himself from the chessboard of whatever game her mother had foreseen. "I do not want to meet him at all. I am glad our association is ended. The interviews were terrible to suffer through."

"But you were there to ensure propriety was maintained. Was he really so rude to the unfortunate ladies?" Seraphina folded up the letter and placed it on the edge of the desk.

He was rude, but the fault had not been his alone. Hannah had betrayed Miss Knightley's confidence. And then there was Lady Gabriella Ridlington, who treated Hannah as though she were a member of staff.

She brushed a hand over the cotton apron that protected her day dress, plucking at the durable fabric. "He was not the worst of it. Lady Gabriella made cruel remarks about my wardrobe."

Pages in the large book turned as her mother returned to the more current generations. "Let her obsess over fripperies. We both know there are more important things in life than a frock."

Hannah left her mother's side to stare out the window. From up here, she could see the stream flowing down the side of their property. Willows dipped their graceful limbs and trailed tips that created small eddies. Beyond, like flecks of cream, sheep grazed in the meadows.

A sigh ran through her body as hot tears pricked at her eyes. Why did she always have to concentrate on the important things in life? Was she never to be allowed a few moments to skim the shallower waters?

"It's not like you to get upset over a dress, Hannah. Will you tell me what truly pained you about her words?" The wheels of the bath chair squeaked as her mother turned the contraption to face her daughter.

She fisted her hands in the apron. "Is it so wrong to want a beautiful dress? There are many women like me, plain creatures who will never bask in the light of adoration. But we still yearn to know, if only fleetingly, what it feels like to think ourselves beautiful. When you spend your entire life on the edge of the shadows, all you can think of is one glorious moment to feel the warm caress of the sun."

She closed her eyes and willed away the tears. Silly to want something so far out of reach. But wasn't that the way of life? People always coveted what they lacked.

"Hannah." Her mother spoke her name with such a mingling of love and pain. "Do you know how it grieves a mother to not be able to soothe every pain her child suffers?"

"I am sorry, Mother. I did not mean to trouble you." Hannah tried to smile as she threw herself down where her mother's feet should have rested.

"Beauty is not found in a pretty dress, but in the reflection in the eyes of those who love you." Seraphina lifted her veil, like the bride at the end of the marriage ceremony who anticipates the groom's kiss. She flicked the muslin over her head and her gloved hands raised Hannah's face. "What do you see when you look upon me?"

Hannah clasped her hands tight as she knelt

before her mother, but she didn't flinch or look away. "I see the powerful mage who gave me life, the mother who loves me unconditionally, and the woman who would do anything for her family."

A smile pulled on thin grey lips. "You don't see the rotting cadaver, then? Perhaps you need spectacles, my dear. My flesh is separating from the bone around my eye sockets and there is blue putrefaction spreading across my cheeks."

Hannah placed one hand on the arm of the bath chair. "You are my mother and I love you."

"Exactly my point, dearest. While others would look at me and recoil in horror, you do not. Your father looks at me and sees the woman in the bloom of youth, with dewy skin and sparkling eyes, who stormed the court and demanded her full due as a mage. Ask me how I know that." The smile broadened on her mother's face. Hannah almost forgot that no blood pulsed through her body, as mischief gave her mother another sort of life.

"How do you know that is what he sees?" Hannah whispered.

"Because that is the reflection I see in his gaze. True beauty is in how others see you, not in a garment you wear." Having said her piece, Seraphina pulled the veil over her dead face. "We simply need to find a man intelligent enough to see that you are beautiful on both the inside and the outside."

"I'd rather talk about puppies. Having given it

some thought, if possible I would like a spaniel with long, silky ears and a chocolate and white coat." A dog would love unconditionally. It didn't matter if she were short or tall, voluptuous or thin. A dog's reflection would show her what her mother spoke of.

Seraphina tapped the end of her daughter's nose. "You can thumb your nose at love, but it might just creep up on you one day."

"Set a puppy behind me and it will. Now, enough talk of irrelevant things—we have work to do."

The day progressed as Hannah worked through the names in the book. Less than one name in ten proved to be that of an aftermage. They had enough to commence their study, but it would be a very small group with no more than five. They would need to hold some aftermages' brains in reserve if Unwin and Alder obtained fewer than ten a month.

As Hannah separated the names into groups, another part of her mind gnawed over numbers. Her father had taught her to ask the questions that nibbled in the shadows of thoughts. That often her subconscious mind had seen something that had not yet occurred to her conscious self.

Two hundred people had attended Lizzie's ball. The *ton* comprised the upper ten thousand peers. Three hundred pots of face powder had been sold to nobles. Two hundred women relied on Unwin and Alder to fulfil their needs.

Her concern finally took shape and allowed her to voice it aloud. "The numbers don't add up. Where are the missing Afflicted?"

"What do you mean, dearest?" Her mother closed the enormous genealogy tome.

Hannah had learned much on her visit to the resurrectionists. "Unwin and Alder have two hundred Afflicted as clients. We know that there were three hundred containers of face powder sold to members of the *ton*, of which Father has five locked up in his laboratory. That leaves us with ninety-five unaccounted for."

Her mother drummed her fingers above the book as though she counted in the air. "There will be a number of Afflicted who do not rely upon the services of Unwin and Alder. Some people may have shared a pot. I believe there are sisters who were both infected from the same container of powder. Then there will be some containers that were never used and so no one was ever struck down. Like the container that languished on a courtesan's dressing table."

Even assuming some pots remained unopened and others were responsible for multiple infections, the available facts still didn't add up. "I cannot imagine that so many would go unused when it was an expensive and sought-after luxury. Nor was a double infection commonplace."

Her mother's hands stilled. "Your father and I

believe there are others who were buried before the extent of the contamination was known. Then, for whatever reason, they were not dug up."

Hannah shivered as she imagined the women waking, only to find themselves imprisoned in coffins. Dead, yet still conscious and abandoned to a terrible fate by their families. How long did they fight to escape before the rot or hunger overcame them?

An idea too horrifying to contemplate wormed its way to the front of Hannah's thoughts. What if they were dealing with an unidentified Afflicted who was feeding on Londoners? A madwoman, or madman, who could strike at any time at any one? A murderer who could not be stopped by normal means? Hannah did know where a few of the unaccounted-for Afflicted resided: in an undisclosed location her father travelled to once a week, to check on those who were interred. Knowing their numbers might allay her growing fear. "How many are held for the safety of England?"

Seraphina held up one hand and wriggled each covered digit. "Two committed murder and another three were identified as being unsafe, and removed. That gave us three men and two women who could not control their hunger and who had to be interred. Then there were another five women who could not reconcile what they had become with their religious beliefs. They have refused to allow any brain matter to pass their lips and your father closely monitors their condition."

"Only three men infected, and they were all unable to control themselves. What does that say about us?" Ten in total and still short of the ninety-odd who were ghosts in her thoughts. Her father had always denied her requests to study them, but she would ask again, as they had much to learn. She was no delicate gentlewoman, and the more they learned the more they would have to analyse.

"We women have always been better at ignoring our needs and moderating our appetites," Seraphina mused. "It is no easy thing to do what we must, to keep ourselves ambulatory. Each individual must decide for themselves if they can consume the brain of another. For myself, I find comfort in knowing a donor lived their allotted years on this earth and have no further use for their mind. Unwin and Alder see to it that their families receive payment for what we need and for some, that coin might save the entire family from starving and meeting a too early end."

Hannah steeled her spine. "Then we have two extremes. Those who refuse the slivers of matter and those who cannot devour enough. Yet both types have met the same end. Father has long denied my request to study them, but I will not be protected any longer." For too long Hannah had lived a quiet life, doing as instructed. No longer would she be blown by the winds of fate; she would navigate her own course. She tried to pierce the veil covering her mother's face to gauge whether she would agree with her request or not.

"It would seem some of Viscount Wycliff's rebelliousness has rubbed off on you. But I agree with you, Hannah. We have protected you and tried to shield you from the worst of life, for that is what a parent does. But you are a child no longer and deserve to be a full partner in this endeavour." Seraphina reached out and stroked the side of Hannah's face.

"A child no more," Hannah murmured. What would Viscount Wycliff think of that? "But may I still have a puppy?"

## 19

Hannah clenched her hands around the notebook as she sat in the carriage. With her mother's support, they had both tackled Sir Hugh over lunch and insisted that she be allowed to study the interred Afflicted. A tickle at the back of her mind wondered if there was something to be learned of their unknown murderer by studying those with no control over their impulses.

While her father assured her that none had escaped, part of her needed to confirm with her own eyes that they were all present and accounted for. With a deranged murderer on the loose, one couldn't be too careful.

In a rare example of *be careful what you wish for* in action, her father announced he could take her immediately, as he had his regular rounds to do. Once she recovered from the shock of getting her own way, Hannah dashed upstairs for a bonnet and a long sage-green pelisse to protect against the cooler weather. Next she went to the library and chose a fresh notebook, tucking a pencil down the spine. She intended to make her own notes and observations to mull over later.

Nerves activated in her stomach as they drew closer to their destination. What would she find—mindless monsters in the grip of addiction screaming for brains? Or sad, still corpses?

They did not have far to journey. The secure location was midway between Craven Hill and Westbourne Green. They turned off the dirt road and the carriage rolled under a tall, wrought-iron gate. The gatekeeper saluted to the driver as they passed and closed the gates with a clang behind them.

Goosebumps erupted along Hannah's arms under her pelisse. They had passed through a magical barrier. She peered out the window, but nothing appeared out of the ordinary.

A short, curved driveway deposited them in front of a two-storey house that squatted into its surrounds. A cropped lawn ran from the house to a high wall that enclosed the property and gave the impression that it held tight the secrets it contained.

She glanced up at the house's stern exterior. Thick windows in mullioned frames obscured any view inside. Apart from the man who had emerged from the gatehouse, there was no one else about. The house was enveloped in an eerie cloud that made the hairs on the back of her neck prickle. There was more than one spell at work here.

Hannah hugged the notebook closer to her chest and wished she had brought a larger one, or one with a metal cover, to make a more effective shield.

"What is this place?" she asked her father.

"It is known as the Repository of Forgotten Things," he replied. "All you need know is that it is owned by the Home Office and used to house things best kept secret."

A tingle made a slow journey down her spine. "I sense Mother's touch here."

Her father glanced sideways at her. "Seraphina has ensorcelled the bricks of both the outer walls and the house to ensure the secrets held here stay contained."

The secrets...or the residents?

They stepped into the embrace of the front porch. The door was set back three feet and created a nook where a person could shelter from the weather while waiting to gain admittance.

Sir Hugh withdrew a key from his jacket pocket and unlocked the door.

Hannah hesitated before she followed her father in. She stared at the toe of her boot as she trod over the threshold, as though she stepped from one world to another. Her senses were on the alert for other enchantments she might encounter.

The hall was large enough for a side table, a bench, and a hat stand. Before them, stairs marched straight up to meet a landing for the second floor. The walls were encased in dark panelling and rugs of deep green were laid over the floorboards. The small dimensions of the space and dark colours made it feel as though they stood in a mossy cavern.

There were no sounds of life or occupants. The only noise was the tick of the clock standing guard against the wall. Hannah had expected the bustling activity of a military camp or a hospital. Instead, the house held the silence of a library or a church.

"This way, Hannah," her father said as he led the way down the hall.

If Hannah strained her ears, she could catch the shuffle of feet or a muffled cough from behind closed doors they passed. Curiosity made her wish to peer through keyholes, but she had to keep pace with her father's long stride.

At the end of the hall was a set of stairs leading downward. Lanterns attached along the wall held flames that appeared frozen in time—they gave off a constant light but never flickered with a breeze, nor did they burn down.

Sir Hugh paused at the top step, his hand on the railing. "Prepare yourself, Hannah. Some of the interred are not pleasant to observe, being in an advanced state of decay."

"Are they not fed sufficiently to keep it at bay?" It had not occurred to her to question how they were fed. Although given the fact that two were murderers, they did not deserve any more than the equivalent of a prison ration.

He shook his head. "The Repository houses those who could not control their appetites. Even gluttony is not enough to sustain them. But you will see for yourself."

She was no stranger to rot. Like her father, she had adopted the Afflicted cause and had seen what it did to women on the outside and the inside. "Do they remain conscious?"

"Some, yes." He said no more, and then began the descent.

At the bottom of the stairs was another hallway. This one had metal doors, rather than wooden. The magical lights were again encased in tiny glass and metal prisons. A chill washed over Hannah's skin beneath her gown and pelisse. The shiver of magic in use combined with the bite of a chill spring day worked through to her bones.

A man in a black uniform sat at a small table at the end of the hall. A sword hung at his side. A ring of heavy keys rested on the table, along with an open book. A rifle leaned against the wall. He stood upon seeing them.

"Afternoon, Sir Hugh," he said.

Sir Hugh nodded in his direction. "Afternoon, Fallon. This is my daughter, Hannah. She will be assisting me from now on. Is there anything to report?"

The soldier bowed to Hannah. "Afternoon, miss. Nothing to report, sir. Let me know when you are ready to begin."

Hannah closed her eyes and concentrated, sorting through what at first seemed a strange hum. When she placed the noise, she opened her eyes. "They're moaning."

"Some moan, others growl. And a few are silent despite what they endure." Her father approached a door and drew a bolt that held a metal shutter in place. He pulled it open and peered within. Then he closed the window and waved to Fallon. "We shall start here, please."

The soldier slung his rifle over his shoulder and picked up the keys. He selected one and unlocked the door, which opened with a ghostly whisper. The room was small at barely eight feet square. Each side had a built-in bench that could double as a bed. Hanging upside down from the ceiling was an ensorcelled mushroom like the one Hannah had in her bedroom. A soft yellow glow bathed the occupant of the cell.

The unfortunate woman lay on one of the hard benches with no blanket or pillow. Her arms were crossed over her chest, as though she were an Egyptian princess awaiting mummification. Or one who had been recently unwrapped. Her body was clad in a bleached linen shift that was far too large for her and it drooped scandalously low from one shoulder.

She was in an advanced state of decay. No flesh or muscle remained. She was bones and tendons encased in tight skin that resembled leather. Only wisps of hair clung to her scalp. She appeared dead, except her jaw moved as she whispered to herself.

"Good afternoon, Lady Jessope. I have brought my daughter, Hannah, to visit. I thought you might like a little feminine company for a change." Sir Hugh set his black bag on the floor and picked up the desiccated corpse's hand.

"How do you do, Lady Jessope?" The name was vaguely familiar, but Hannah had never met the woman while she lived. Hannah bobbed a small curtsey and then pulled out her notebook and pencil. She drew a sketch of the other woman, noting the tendons visible through torn skin and the position of arms and legs.

"How are you today, Lady Jessope? Do you require any sustenance?" Sir Hugh asked.

"No." The tongue worked to push out the word, its action visible through splits in the throat.

Once he completed his examination, Sir Hugh

ushered Hannah from the room and the soldier locked the door behind them.

"Did she mummify naturally, or was the process created artificially?" Hannah asked as soon as the solid door was closed.

"It occurred naturally. As you saw, the decay consumed all the soft tissue and most of the internal organs. The skin and tendons hardened until they took on the consistency of tanned hide or leather." Her father's eyes lit up as he described the process.

"Most of her internal organs—what remains?" Hannah digested the information and scribbled notes on the page.

"Her heart. It is just visible through a tear between her upper ribs. All the other organs followed the normal course of putrefaction, and liquified and leaked from her body. But her heart has been mummified in a way similar to that of her skin and tendons. It has been perfectly preserved and remains, like a small leather ball, in her chest."

"Why does the heart remain in this instance, and yet the maid ceased being ambulatory when hers rotted?" Hannah pondered aloud. "Granted, the Afflicted have no heartbeat, but it would seem to indicate that the organ has a vital role in their continued consciousness."

"An excellent hypothesis, Hannah." Sir Hugh beamed and patted her arm.

"Was Lady Jessope a voluntary interment? I

cannot imagine the strength of will it would take to refuse sustenance while your flesh falls from your bones." Hannah added a brief history to the sketch.

"Yes. We have five such Afflicted here, all very devout women." Her father gestured to four other doors along the corridor.

"Will she be buried when she is no longer conscious?" If the heart did not beat and support the circulation of blood, then what function was it performing? Hannah recalled something of the Egyptian belief that the heart was the seat of the soul. She wrote a note next to the drawing of Lady Jessope to remind her to discuss the possibility with her mother.

The dark curse used might have had an Egyptian origin.

"Her husband has a seat in the House of Lords and requests a weekly report of her health. Unlike some nobles, Lord Jessope retains affection for his wife." Sir Hugh gestured for the soldier to unlock the next door.

"Such a lonely existence for them." Those with fervent beliefs expected upon their deaths to be heralded by angels and borne up to sit at the feet of God. Not to be imprisoned in a basement outside of London.

"We did try putting them in together, but they became very agitated. Each woman is calmer alone, without the visible reminder of what she has become.

They spend their time in prayer. I suppose their lives are not dissimilar to those in some monastic orders."

They visited the other four women, all in peaceful repose. One clutched a rosary between her dried fingers, her tight, shrivelled lips murmuring the Hail Mary over and over.

"What of the other five? The ones who could not control their appetites?" Hannah counted metal doors. There were five on one side of the corridor and only three on the other. What lurked behind each one?

Her father's expression became serious, his eyebrows pulled slightly down and toward one another. "They are not as peaceful to observe. They are dangerous, Hannah."

"I'm ready, Father. I would know the full extent of what we seek to cure."

Sir Hugh gestured to Fallon, the guard. He unlocked a small steel door by his table. From inside he withdrew a glass preserving jar. From a nearby shelf he retrieved five wooden bowls. With a pair of tongs, he extracted a slice of matter from the jar and placed one in each bowl.

When the jar was locked away again, he stacked the bowls one on top of another and passed them to Sir Hugh. Next, he unlocked the door at the end of the hallway.

Screams escaped and washed over Hannah.

"Stay to the right of the room, my dear. Do not

step within arm's reach, for they will lunge for you," her father warned over the shrieks and cries.

Hannah hugged the notebook tighter and followed her father and the soldier inside. The next room was more bleak prison block than quiet monastery cell. A short corridor ran along the front of five small cells, and a wooden bench was placed against the far wall. Stone walls kept the prisoners apart and stout iron bars separated them from those who cared for them.

The cries rose to an angry pitch. Bars rattled as fingers curled around the iron. The sharp tang of rot assaulted Hannah's nose.

"They have not mummified." She peered around her father at the occupant of the first cell. In life, he had been a tall man. In death, he was a nightmare made real.

Rot consumed his soft tissue, but it fell in droplets on the ground around him. Liquified internal organs oozed down his side from a gash in his skin. His skin tore in random spots across his body. A split in his cheek revealed the action of his tongue as it wagged against his teeth.

When he spotted Hannah, he jumped to the bars and stuck an arm through as far as he could, swiping and clawing at her.

Sir Hugh moved Hannah to the extreme right and well beyond their reach. "These Afflicted each receive their daily sliver. However, we have observed that the ration that keeps all the other Afflicted in a stable condition is insufficient for these five and they continue to decay. I hypothesise that hunger is linked to the cycle of decay and healing. They cannot control their hunger—likewise, the rot is uncontrolled."

An idea flared into life. There was a clue in how, for these Afflicted, their constant appetite was linked to the more rapid decay. She just needed to puzzle out why. Hannah wrestled her senses under control. The ear-piercing screams, the suffocating smell, and the visual horror assaulted her in every way, but she stood her ground. "The others seemed so peaceful. By comparison, this is...horrific. Imagine if they shuffled down the Strand. People would panic."

"Not only from their appearance. They would dash open the skulls of the living and tear out their brains while their hearts still beat, and we know the tragic effect of that."

Those secondary creatures were additionally cursed: the lack of brains made them shambling monsters intent on death. When identified, those deceased were cremated and their ashes interred in lead boxes and buried before they could be reanimated.

Hannah drew in her notebook, to capture the misery and horror caged before her. "The actions of our murderer are similar to these Afflicted. Yet the person responsible cannot have such a terrifying countenance. Such an Afflicted would be easily discovered."

Sir Hugh patted the bowls in his arms. "Remember, these five are fed the same diet that is sufficient to maintain the others who retain their places in society. If these five ate an entire brain every few days, it is entirely possible they would look just like anyone else. Perhaps even with a flush of health to their skin."

Conversation was difficult over the screams and cries. Instead, Hannah wrote notes to follow up with her father later, in the peace of the carriage. What was it about these five that made a sliver a day insufficient to maintain them? Could it be as simple as a deficit of character, an innate weakness that made them more susceptible to gluttony?

Fallon picked up what appeared to be a type of shovel, the end being flat and square. Sir Hugh placed a bowl on the end and then the soldier slid the shovel and bowl under the bars. The Afflicted fell upon the bowl. The process was repeated at each cell. The shouts and screams were replaced by soft murmurs, sighs, and then a slurping noise as the prisoners licked their bowls clean.

"More," one said, and thrust the bowl back through the bars.

The chant of *more* was taken up by the others, as they all held out their bowls. Requests turned pleading and then angry. The single word was screamed at Hannah and the others. She pressed herself against the brick wall as she sat on the bench to continue her drawing. Hannah quickly sketched the closest Afflicted, arm stretched through the bars as he waved the bowl and screamed for his hunger to be sated.

Even as she drew, his body sought to heal. Rips in skin stuck themselves back together. His flesh evened out and the constant seep of foul-smelling liquid stopped.

Her father took a seat next to her.

"Have you tried feeding them more? If nothing else, it would keep the rot at bay." Hannah added bars to her drawing, keeping the monster safely contained.

"We did try in the beginning. Like opium addicts, we found they required an ever-increasing amount simply to sustain the same level of repair. At one point they were being fed an entire brain a week, and yet they still decayed at an accelerated rate."

"Fascinating," Hannah murmured. The curse did not progress the same way in every victim. If they could determine why, it might aid their search for a cure.

She couldn't help but think of the calm that wrapped itself around Lady Jessope and her fellow disciples. Their self-denial resulted in the curse mummifying their bodies and keeping them conscious. In the other five, their gluttony resulted in their bodies dripping with rot while an insatiable hunger demanded more. It was as though the beliefs of the sufferer dictated the course of the affliction.

Before her were the only male Afflicted, three men raging and screaming at the bars holding them captive. Her mother said that Sir Ewan Shaw had been shot by a French officer they suspected to be Afflicted. From his description, the Frenchman had not been a shambling nightmare like these men. What if there were other men who were Afflicted, but who had not succumbed like the ones before her?

Was it possible that the murderer Viscount Wycliff sought was a man, able to move through society without any knowing of his deceased state? A male Afflicted could hide among members of society as the Frenchman moved among his fellow troops, and only his larger appetite would give him away.

## 20

Wycliff stood on the corner and waited for a phaeton and pair to clatter past. As one day turned into another, his investigation into the murdered cloakroom attendant made little progress. He had spent two days ratting around in the man's life and hadn't found anyone with so much as a harsh thing to say about him.

A young boy next to him clutched an armload of scandal sheets. The lad waved one at Wycliff. "Read all about it, sir. Gruesome murderer on the loose!"

Wycliff shook his head as he carried on his way home. Lady Miles had set free a greater rumour to counteract the murder during the Loburn ball, but two gruesome murders couldn't be ignored. The last thing they needed was publicity about the Afflicted's habits that would panic the population. No Londoner would feel safe if they thought a well-bred lady were circling behind them with a canapé fork in hand.

He had proposed to Sir Manly Powers that all the Afflicted be rounded up and kept in a secure location until their culprit revealed herself by her actions. That had not been well received, even though it would protect the ordinary people of London. Yet again, those with power and influence dictated the course of events.

His hands curled into fists. He would discover the murderer and then perhaps those higher up would finally see reason. Nobles should be treated no differently than the common born. Wealth and position should never be used as a shield with which to escape justice.

Today, Wycliff headed to the home of Lord Albright. While Albright might not have direct knowledge of the murderer, it was a noteworthy coincidence that two murders had occurred at events he attended. There was a slender chance the man could help Wycliff better understand any potential motives of his previous wife. Finding a motive for the murders might then reveal the person responsible.

Albright was not at home, but his butler directed Wycliff to a local mews, where his lordship was inspecting a new purchase. Wycliff approached the stables with a lighter step. He had managed to keep hold of his horse. He should have sold the mare to pay down his father's debt with a blacklegs at the racetrack, but couldn't part with his sensitive and responsive mount. Life had taken so much from him already that he clung to the quiet joy found in riding the horse.

Horses had a soothing presence and the rhythm of their breathing made him take deep, steadying breaths. They were much like dogs and didn't care a whit for a man's title or pocketbook. They judged a man on his actions and how he treated them.

The mews bustled with activity as some horses were ridden out, and others were mucked out. A row stood waiting to be shod by the brawny smith working in an open yard. The ring of metal hitting cobbles mingled with equine snorts and soft human conversation.

Wycliff held out a hand to a dark bay tied to a rail, patiently waiting to be shod. The gelding snuffled at his glove and nibbled the leather. He scratched the horse's neck as he peered into the wide breezeway, looking for Lord Albright. He found him running his hand over a leggy grey mare.

Albright was in his fifties and cut a trim figure. Probably to draw attention away from the fact that his hair had vanished like grass during a drought. When he bent over to examine the horse's hoof, the light played over his bald head. His face was defined by sharp cheekbones and a narrow jaw, with small lips that made him look perpetually annoyed.

As Wycliff walked into the stable, he inhaled the

sweet aroma of hay and horse. Why didn't women use such scents to attract a man, instead of cloying perfumes that assaulted the nostrils with all the subtlety of a cavalry charge?

"You have a handsome creature there, Albright." Miss Miles was uppermost in his mind and to appease her memory, he tried a more relaxed approach rather than thrusting in with a direct question.

Albright looked up and grunted. "She should be, for the amount she cost. Saddle her up, I'll take her out myself today." He gestured to the waiting groom and slapped the mare on the rump. "If you think I know anything about these murders, you are mistaken."

Wycliff watched the horse led away and resisted the urge to sigh like a deprived child. "Actually, I wanted to discuss your wife."

The man's upper lip pulled back in a sneer. "I assume you mean my former and now *deceased* wife." The reminder of his previous wife evoked a physical response in Albright. Invective flowed into his mouth and flew past his lips as spittle when he spoke.

"Indeed." Wycliff moved out of spitting range and leaned on a stall door. "Did you converse with her at either the Loburn ball or The Harriers?"

The man's eyes widened and he inhaled sharply. "Felicity is dead. I don't converse with her at all and I am kept much occupied by my lovely *present* wife and children, all of whom possess a pulse. To address your question, I did see her at Loburn's with that ridiculous black veil, but I had no idea she was at The Harriers."

Wycliff waited while a stable boy wheeled a cart of manure along the aisle. "She told me she wished to talk to you, but went no farther than the entrance. Do you think your former wife capable of murderous intent?"

Albright snorted. "Highly improbable. The woman was like tepid porridge while alive—bland and easily forgotten. I never once heard her raise her voice or saw her display any passion for life."

A description that dovetailed with Miss Miles's assessment of the late Lady Albright. Although Miss Miles had worded it more delicately. "Then what matter do you think she wants to pursue with you?"

The groom returned with the saddled horse and Albright ran a hand under the girth. "I have no idea. She is none of my concern any longer."

The man dropped his responsibilities with remarkable ease. Wycliff wasn't so sure he could turn his back on someone who had once shared his bed and home. Even the dead needed somewhere to rest their bones and someone to safeguard their eternal sleep. "No concern at all? You married her and vowed to honour and cherish her."

"My vows were until death us did part. Felicity

died. What was I supposed to do, share my home with a corpse?" Albright's eyes narrowed and the flow of spittle increased with his agitation. The horse danced sideways and the groom at her head tightened his grip on the reins.

Wycliff thought that was exactly what some did. A woman's lack of pulse didn't preclude her from contributing to daily family life. He only had to consider the guest list for the Loburn ball to see that a number of the Afflicted had been included in the celebration, despite their deceased status.

"If I might enquire, how did you become aware of the late Lady Albright's condition?" Wycliff pitched his voice low, as though he spoke to the nervous horse. He didn't want Albright bolting before he dug a little deeper. The voice in the back of his head said this was a thread worth chasing.

"I assume she bought herself one of those jars of fancy face powder, trying to look younger. Then she sickened and died, much like many other women. Felicity's cousin insisted I delay the funeral to allow distant relatives from the countryside time to reach London. I said I didn't want her body at my house, and so she was laid out at her cousin's."

From the rumours Wycliff had heard, the new wife had been secured and moved in before the old was even cold. All of London knew his new wife had delivered a healthy full-term heir just four months after the hasty wedding.

There would have been quite the scene if the two wives had met in the parlour when one was resurrected. Chaos had resulted in homes around London as mourners saw the deceased apparently revive before them. A miracle that, over the passage of weeks, revealed itself as being instead a nightmarish curse. "So the late Lady Albright regained consciousness at her cousin's?"

Albright's hand tightened into a fist around his riding crop as he waited for a lad to lengthen the stirrups. "Yes. I should have kept a tighter grip on events. Then I could have ensured she was properly buried and not free to haunt my waking moments."

Wycliff wasn't entirely sure he understood the other man's meaning. "You would have buried her *after* her revival?"

Albright glanced toward the grooms and then leaned in close to Wycliff. "Do you think I would have been the only man to inter a troublesome wife who didn't have the dignity to go quietly to death? I was just bloody unlucky that others saw her sit up. Otherwise she would have been dispatched to her grave to leave the living in peace."

Wycliff's stomach clenched. Albright's words exactly reflected Wycliff's own views and thoughts on the matter of the Afflicted. Yet to hear his innermost thoughts voiced by another man made them seem...wrong. The dead deserved to rest. What peace would there be for women forced into coffins and buried in the ground while they screamed and clawed at the unyielding wood? Perhaps Miss Miles was right to argue that they be allowed to exist undisturbed...so long as they obeyed English law and didn't dine on the servants.

Wycliff recalled a soft patch of lawn with Hannah Miles at her mother's feet while the two women chatted as though one were not a rotting piece of flesh. The young woman spoke with respect of her mother and treated the Afflicted as though they were any other breathing person. Had he been wrong all along, and a person actually retained their soul beyond death?

Albright nodded to the groom, who laced his hands and provided a stirrup to lift him into the saddle. He gathered up the reins and then flicked out the tails of his jacket.

Wycliff stepped back. "You have been most helpful, Albright. If you do recollect anything about your former wife that might be of assistance, do pass it along to me."

Albright nodded and put heel to the mare, trotting out of the mews and along the road.

Wycliff left in a thoughtful mood. His beliefs had been challenged by hearing them from another's lips and as he walked, he re-examined his interactions with the Afflicted women.

As he neared his rented home, he considered his options. If Lord Albright didn't think his former wife capable of murder, that left two viable suspects—Emma Knightley and Gabriella Ridlington. But how to flush the right prey from the undergrowth where they hid from him?

As he approached his front door, a man on the pavement hailed him. He vaguely recognised him as being one of the Bow Street Runners who investigated the everyday crimes that plagued the streets of London.

"My lord, the magistrate sent me to tell you about a stiff we pulled out of the river the other week." He took off his cloth cap and clenched it between his fingers.

Ah. Finally his request for any information about similar murders in London had yielded an answer. "Was the body missing its brain?"

The man nodded, then glanced around and waited for a couple to pass before continuing. "Head was bashed in and the skull was empty. He'd been in the Thames for a few days before we pulled him out and we just assumed fish had been at him. They tend to nibble on bodies thrown in the water."

Fish were a distinct possibility. But so was an Afflicted with an appetite to satisfy. "When was this?"

The man screwed up his face as he thought. "Three weeks ago?"

That would make three such deaths within the space of three weeks, assuming the same hand had emptied all three skulls. Excitement built inside him. This could be the pivotal piece of information he needed. "And where did you fish him out?"

The man gestured off toward the east. "Over at the West India docks. We asked around and from all accounts, he was an argumentative bugger and probably picked a fight with the wrong person. Happens a lot around there."

Damn. No fine lady would be wandering around the docks at night. The murder might not be connected at all if fish were responsible for the missing brain. But this was the first similar crime his questions had uncovered. "Thank you. You have been most helpful."

As Wycliff approached his door, he pondered how a murder at the wharf could be related to two in more civilised surroundings. Then one thought crashed through his mind. There was a new business at those docks. A high-end business that supplied the *ton*. Rowley and Sons, importers of French champagne.

He called out to the Runner before he disappeared along the road. "One more thing. Did you identify the corpse?"

The man tugged his cap back on his head. "Oh, yes. He worked for Rowley and Sons. Is that all, my lord?"

"Yes. Thank you." Such was his gratitude that he tossed the man a coin he could ill afford to give.

While a theory coalesced in his mind, he pushed into his house and picked up the assortment of envelopes on the hall table. One was a notice from his landlord, giving him until the end of the week to vacate the premises. The eviction was not unexpected. The rent was just one of many bills he had neglected as he sought to satisfy his father's debtors.

He walked through to his cold front parlour and tossed the letters into the grate. At least the invoices were good for something. He would use them to start a fire tonight.

He leaned one hand on the mantel while he stared at the scattered papers. Miss Miles might have been justified in her defence of the women Afflicted. He was beginning to suspect they were not responsible. Or at least not directly. For there was one deceased woman who had a connection with Rowley and Sons.

Lady Gabriella Ridlington.

Suspicions and theories would never satisfy his superior, especially not when members of the *ton* were involved. He needed proof, or even better, a confession.

Afternoon edged toward evening as he set out in search of Lady Gabriella and her beau, Mr Jonathon Rowley. He tried the most obvious place first—the large and imposing mansion in Mayfair.

The butler opened the door and then threw down the gauntlet for a staring competition. It would seem the lady in question had been quite adamant when she'd said she didn't want to see Wycliff again. The infuriating guard dog at the door wasn't going to admit him.

"I can come back with soldiers and force entry," he informed the man. "Before I seek reinforcements, perhaps you could answer a simple question. Is Lady Gabriella at home?"

The butler narrowed his eyes and pursed his lips. "No, my lord. My lady has departed for the evening."

"Where has she gone?"

"That I am not at liberty to say. Good evening." The solid door was slammed shut in his face.

"Damn it!" He pounded his fist into the brick by the door. If not for his glove, he would have removed a layer of skin from his knuckles.

This butler might be paid for his silence, but he would wager someone in the Rowley household would know where the prodigal son had gone.

**21**

---

Hannah was curled up in the library window seat with a book when Mary peered around the door.

"One of the Marquess of Loburn's men is here for you, miss." The maid held out an envelope.

Hannah placed a bookmark on the page and closed the book before taking the note. It was from her beloved Elizabeth. "Lizzie wants my company this evening."

Part of her wanted to refuse. Two social outings in one month? That was unheard of for Hannah. She simply didn't have the mental stamina to withstand the barbs thrown by Lizzie's peers. But there was the annoying itch that had formed at the back of her mind after what she had seen at her father's Repository of Forgotten Things.

Her mother said her gift was the ability to place

herself in someone else's shoes. That was easy to do with Emma Knightley. As they were both the only child of devoted parents, she could imagine all parties involved would do anything for the happiness of the others.

But she baulked at putting herself in Lady Gabriella's shoes, even if they were exquisitely embroidered silk ones. Such a shallow and vain creature. Hannah saw no appeal in understanding her situation. Given the sharpness of her tongue and her Afflicted status, despite her wealth and title, Hannah could only imagine her shoes would convey a sense of loneliness with each step.

*Loneliness!* Her mind leapt on that word. Lady Gabriella was a woman uncomfortable on her own. She needed an audience to admire her beauty, her clothes, or her latest verbal barb. To what lengths would she go in order to ensure she did not see out her days alone?

Hannah shuddered at the implications, but her theory needed to be conveyed to Lord Wycliff. Since the murders, the wraith had taken to haunting social gatherings. Lizzie said he lurked in the shadows, no doubt waiting to pounce on the murderer. There was a good chance he might also be present this evening, and Hannah wanted to tell him why she believed him to be wrong in his identification of the murderer as one of the female Afflicted. Something within her whispered it could be a male Afflicted.

Hannah glanced at the large clock that hung above the fireplace. The hands told her that dusk had only begun to fall outside, dinner was still an hour away, and there was plenty of time for a young woman to make plans for the evening. Decision made, Hannah dropped the note on top of her book.

"I shall attend, Mary. Please tell the man I'll be along shortly."

"Yes, miss. We'll have you dressed in no time." Mary had a wide smile on her face. The maid enjoyed using her skills at hairdressing, and studied the newspapers and magazines to find the latest fashions. Hannah's going out was a rare opportunity for her to practice the newest styles.

With Mary's able assistance, Hannah was soon clothed in her second-best gown of pale lilac. Small sprigs of lavender were embroidered around the hem and neckline. Her long hair was piled up on top of her head, and wound through with a length of purple ribbon. The sides were secured with two small pins with twinkling diamond stars on the ends.

"You look lovely, miss. Don't know what is wrong with all those young men that they aren't lining up to dance with you." Mary stood back to survey her handiwork.

"You are too kind, Mary. My dance card stays empty because my witty conversation is lacking and young men don't want to be bored with the details of my father's work." Hannah glanced at her image in the mirror, but could only see her faults and how much she lacked compared to the luminous beauties who attracted all the suitors.

Holding in a sigh, she picked up her shawl. How marvellous it would feel to see beauty, or at least admiration for her intelligence, reflected in a man's gaze. A puppy's eyes would show her such things. She should ask Lizzie if any of her friends had spaniel puppies needing new homes.

Her mother awaited her at the bottom of the stairs. Seraphina clasped her hands together. "Oh, I love that shade of purple on."

Hannah brushed at her dress. Compliments made her uncomfortable, even from her mother. "I hear this colour is unfashionable and considered dowdy by some—it is similar to half mourning."

Her mother snorted. "It looks divine on you and if anyone says it is half mourning remind them your mother is dead. Lavender has long been associated with grace, refinement, and intelligence—all things that reflect your nature."

Hannah leaned down and kissed her mother's veiled cheek. "You're my mother. You are obliged to say such things."

Seraphina pressed a slip of paper into Hannah's hand. "Keep this close. I don't like the idea of you encountering the Afflicted responsible for these heinous crimes."

Hannah glanced at the scrap. She recognised the

pattern of the notation, but not the language. "The mouse spell?"

The veil swayed as Seraphina nodded. "Yes, but I used bigger letters so it would work on larger things."

Hannah folded the paper up and tucked it inside her stays, over her heart. "Rest assured, Mother, I have no intention of confronting a murderer. I only want to find Viscount Wycliff and tell him he may be chasing a false scent."

The Loburns' expensive carriage, with its maroon-coloured velvet seats, took Hannah to the marquess's home to collect an exuberant Lady Elizabeth.

Lizzie dropped onto the seat next to Hannah and took her hand. "Oh, Hannah! We will have such fun. Now that I am officially engaged and about to be a married woman, I can finally enjoy myself."

The carriage gave a slight jolt as the horses set off. "Did you not enjoy yourself before becoming engaged? I rather thought you revelled in being surrounded by admiring eligible men."

Lizzie huffed and smoothed a wrinkle in her blush pink gown. "An unattached woman must guard herself every moment to ensure she maintains a demure appearance."

Hannah bit back a snort. She might be a wall-flower, but she never wanted to be demure. If she had an opinion, she would speak it. Why should a woman hold her tongue just because a man could not hold his own in a lively conversation? Hannah would rather remain a spinster than end up trapped in a marriage where she could never voice her innermost thoughts without risking a reprimand from her husband.

Her mother's words floated back to her, when they had discussed the dark days when female mages and aftermages were smothered at birth. A woman with power was the stuff of men's nightmares—yet they thought women the weaker sex.

"There is a reason why I want to attend this party in particular. There is a boy aftermage in the household's employ and rumour has it he can tell whether anything ails a person by touching them. I want to know...that is, if there will be any impediment..." Lizzie's words trailed off as her hand rested over her stomach.

Hannah took her friend's hand. A duchess had many duties, but the most important was to provide her husband with an heir. "You know I will keep any confidence for you. Where will we find this gifted boy?"

Hannah peered out the carriage window. They had not travelled far and were still in Mayfair. The distance was so small they could easily have walked, if it weren't inappropriate for gently bred women to be on the streets at night unescorted. She looked up at the soft golden stone of the house. Lights seemed to blaze in every window and drifts of music wafted out to the driveway.

Lizzie waited for the footman to open the door and offer his assistance to her. "He will be in the stables at the home of Lord Byrd. The soirée is for his daughter's twentieth birthday."

Hannah let Lizzie drag her through the house and toward the ballroom. At one point her friend plucked two glasses of champagne from a silver platter and thrust one into her hand. She hoped that her friend would release her to hold her shawl and reticule as usual. She would rather retreat to the quiet by the walls and observe.

In the packed ballroom, Hannah finally understood Lizzie's mission. Her dashing fiancé was in attendance. The duke's gaze fixed on Lizzie and he pushed through the crowd, ignoring attempts to engage him in conversation as he made a beeline for his beloved.

"Lady Elizabeth, you are the air my lungs need to breathe," the duke said as he took Lizzie's hand and kissed her knuckles.

Lizzie giggled and tapped the duke with her fan. "You are a hopeless romantic, Harden."

"You would inspire the dullest man to poetry with your beauty, my love." He pulled her a little closer and tucked her hand into the crook of his arm.

"I must dance with Harden, Hannah, but I'll not be long, I promise." With pure happiness lighting her angelic face, Lizzie was whisked away by the duke.

A laughing figure in a vibrant red wholly unsuitable for an unmarried woman crossed the floor. Hannah ducked behind a larger woman to avoid the cruel attention of Lady Gabriella Ridlington. Hannah found a quiet spot away from the large doors. She wanted to watch without being jostled while she scanned the crowd for a certain black cloud. Would he be in attendance? It was the first time Hannah had ever hoped to find a particular gentleman at an event. Which of course was a professional interest, not a personal one.

As she tapped a toe to the music, a familiar shape passed by, but not the one she sought. Miss Emma Knightley had her head bowed close to that of a young man wearing a dark green jacket. He ushered her through the doorway. Then he paused, looked back, and gestured to another wearing a maroon waistcoat under his black jacket, who broke away from a group to follow the couple.

Cold slithered down Hannah's gullet. What was going on? She couldn't stay in the ballroom. Even at the risk of missing Wycliff, she had to ascertain whether Miss Knightley was safe.

Hannah passed the task of watching shawl and reticule to a fellow spinster.

"Thank you," Hannah said. As she added Lizzie's silken items to the pile already being safeguarded, it occurred to her that her kind were like dragons, sitting on the pretty items they collected.

That gave birth to an idea for Lizzie's wedding. What if her mother could conjure a dragon to watch over belongings while revellers danced?

Hannah exited the ballroom and started down a long corridor. She had no idea where Miss Knightley and the men might have gone—to a private room, or out into the garden for whatever nefarious thing they were about? She was quite certain it would prove to be something horrid, from the determined look shared by the two young men.

It would be unseemly for her to call out for Miss Knightley. Instead, Hannah crept along the corridor with her ears pricked. The whimper made her pause. From behind a door came a feminine gasp of pain that was followed by the loud bark of a man's laughter.

"Oh, Miss Knightley, whatever are they up to?" Hannah whispered as she approached the source of the sound. Before she lost her courage, she pushed open the door. The tableau inside made her stop in her tracks.

Miss Emma Knightley sat on a chair with her arms outstretched. A young man stood on either side of her, each holding a knife in his hand. The man on the right in the green jacket had stabbed her palm with his knife—the blow that must have elicited the whimper. The other gentleman was in the process of drawing a line down the inside of her forearm. Blood welled in the wake of his blade, then, just as quickly as he cut, her flesh sealed the two edges back together.

"What is going on here?" Hannah demanded. She had wanted to find Miss Knightley, but never imagined to find her being physically tortured.

The men looked up and the one on the right said, "None of your business. Go away."

"This is my business. Miss Knightley is a friend and I will not allow you to harm her."

The one who had spoken, who had pale blond hair gloriously offset by the deep green of his coat, pulled his knife from Emma's hand.

The young woman gasped and gritted her teeth to hold her hand still. Blood dripped onto a handkerchief spread over her lap, no doubt to protect her gown.

*Oh!* Now she understood the scene she'd found the night of the Loburn ball and the stain that had elicited Miss Knightley's tears. Had a similar event happened there and it was her own blood that ruined the dress?

As they watched, the hole in Emma's palm closed as her body sealed the wound.

The young man took a step closer and raised the knife until the tip pointed at Hannah's left eye. "I said, this is none of your business. Now get out, unless you want to join her in amusing us."

His accomplice sniggered.

"I am quite well, Miss Miles. Do not concern yourself." Miss Knightley's voice quavered and told Hannah the opposite.

Concern for Miss Knightley surged through Hannah, along with a dollop of outrage. She was tired of men pushing her around and who did this one think he was, to dare threaten her?

As she stepped closer, the paper her mother had given her scratched against her skin and reminded her that she was never alone. She stiffened her spine and tilted her chin. "How dare you speak to me like that? My mother is Lady Seraphina Miles, once England's premiere mage."

The man sneered. "Your mother is dead."

Hannah met the man's gaze and refused to be cowed. "Yes, and death has not diminished her power, nor her maternal affection. Being Afflicted has released her from the strictures of service to England and she may now wield her power however she sees fit. Spill one drop of my blood and I assure you, there is no place on this earth where you may hide from her wrath."

The man paused for a moment, then threw the blade at the table next to Hannah, making a thud as steel bit into the wood. Then he reached into his pocket, withdrew a coin, and tossed it at Emma's feet. "Come on, Sedley, we've had our sport here. Let's find warm and willing partners for more lively entertainment."

Hannah stared at both men as they left, and waited until the door shut on their backs before rushing to Emma's side. She knelt to examine the wounds in her hand and arm. Both had healed, leaving only the pink glimmer of fresh tissue. It was remarkable how quickly a well-fed Afflicted could repair her injuries.

"Why were you letting those men cut you?" Hannah asked.

Tears glistened in Emma's eyes and she gave a sob. How curious that while the Afflicted did not breathe, they could still succumb to ragged tears. Stilling the heart didn't stop the emotion that produced tears.

"Because they pay me. My parents have so little and I am such a burden. I have discovered that there are men like that...who enjoy cutting me...to watch my body heal the wounds."

"Oh, Emma." Hannah picked up the coin and pressed it into her hand. "It wasn't red wine the night of the Loburn ball, was it? It was indeed blood, but it was your own that you had spilled on your gown."

A tear rolled down Emma's cheek as she nodded silently.

Wycliff was wrong. Again. Miss Knightley was innocent of the crimes he investigated.

"Please don't tell my parents," Emma whispered.

Hannah took her hands in her own. "Of course not. But I would seek your consent to discuss your situation with my father. There may be a way we can keep you supplied with what you need. He is most curious to determine why you do not exhibit signs of rot like the other Afflicted."

The other young woman squeezed her hand. "I would appreciate it if an arrangement could be made. I do so worry about my parents. Now, if you don't mind, I'd like a few moments to myself."

"Of course." Hannah paused midway to the door. "I am so very sorry, too, for the way Lord Wycliff spoke to you, and for my part in the proceedings. I have deeply regretted that day."

The other woman wiped away the tears and managed a weak smile. "Apology accepted. Shall we make a fresh beginning?"

"I would like that. Thank you." With one worry lifted from her shoulders, Hannah left Miss Knightley to collect herself while she gathered her own thoughts in the corridor.

Miss Knightley had a sad secret, but it wasn't a murderous one. She would tell her father when she returned home. Was it possible that the process of cutting and healing herself kept the rot at bay? That it might explain her remarkable condition? Maybe cutting allowed the disease to escape and not ferment within Emma's skin. Thoughts of Egypt and the mummification process once again slipped through Hannah's mind.

Yet running below the rational questions was vindication. She would tell the wraith to his face that he was wrong if she ever—

As she turned a corner she bumped into a dark presence. Hands grabbed her shoulders as she stumbled backwards.

"Miss Miles, what are you doing here?" a rough but familiar voice said.

"You are *wrong*," Hannah blurted, as though he had knocked the words from her.

## 22

Dark brows pulled together as black eyes regarded her. "You came here solely to tell me I am wrong?"

It sounded a tad impertinent when he put it like that. "No, of course not. Lady Elizabeth asked me to accompany her. But I had wanted to speak to you, my lord. I believe your investigation is focused in the wrong direction. Miss Knightley is innocent, and I think there is compelling evidence that a man—"

"Jonathon Rowley is Afflicted," he interrupted.

Hannah swallowed the words on her tongue. *That* wasn't the response she had anticipated. He was supposed to deny her theory and she had a long and convincing argument prepared to make him see that she was right. Now she was the one who needed convincing. "Mr Rowley? How did you arrive at that conclusion?"

His hands dropped from her shoulders, but two warm impressions remained on her skin. "A body was pulled from the Thames three weeks ago, down by the West India docks. It transpires the man worked for Rowley and Sons. Or he did, until someone bashed his head in and removed his brain. What made you suspect a man was responsible?"

"I have seen the Afflicted men who are interred to keep the people of London safe. They are addicted and have ravenous, uncontrollable appetites. My father hypothesised that if such an individual fed frequently enough, he might be indistinguishable from any other living person. At least, while in the early stages of his addiction. But I fear that if Mr Rowley is newly Afflicted, he might not last long." She thought of the body that had lain on her father's autopsy table, and the rotted organ they had found in her chest.

Lord Wycliff's nostrils flared and he ground his teeth. "He will not last past this night if I have anything to do with it. Have you seen either Mr Rowley or Lady Gabriella this evening?"

"I saw them briefly, but I did not wish to cross paths with either."

The viscount cast around the corridor. "We must find them. Given how events unfolded at the Loburn ball and at The Harriers, he will be seeking a private spot and an unwary aftermage servant."

Hannah suddenly remembered the conversation

with Lizzie in the carriage. Apart from seeing her beloved duke, she had had another reason for attending the party. "There is a boy here who is an aftermage, rumoured to be able to diagnose a condition with just a touch."

Hannah wouldn't betray her friend's nervousness over the pressures that would weigh upon her as a newly married duchess. Society and her husband would expect the required heir and spare. Lizzie had hoped the gifted boy might be able to tell if there were any impediment to fulfilling her duty.

Black eyes burned with a cold fire as he stared at her. "Where will we find him?"

We? Lord Wycliff had dismissed her with a terse note. Now he included her in his plan as though she were an equal? Thinking of notes brought to mind her mother's. Hannah might be able to provide practical assistance in apprehending the murderer. Given the coiled energy in the viscount's form, it seemed a better course of action to stay beside him and not in his path. "I understand the boy can be found at the stables."

Wycliff grabbed her hand and pulled her along with him. Along the corridor they raced, toward the back of the house. Liveried servants squawked and dodged out of their way like ruffled chickens.

They burst from the back of the house into a courtyard. Down wide stone steps the viscount tugged Hannah, and across the cobbles that stretched from house to stables. A mist had descended with the night, and the air seemed close. The lanterns gave only small circles of light as though they struggled to penetrate the inky darkness.

"There!" Hannah spied a flutter of deep red silk that caressed the corner of the building and then disappeared from sight. Lady Gabriella was wearing such a dress. They were close to their quarry.

Wycliff plowed around the side of the barn. At the rear, a small addition butted up against the stables. The side they approached had no windows, only a rough-hewn door. A muffled cry came from inside, then a thud.

"Hit him again!" Lady Gabriella's voice hissed and escaped through gaps in the building like steam from a kettle.

Without pausing, the viscount threw himself shoulder first into the door. Wood splintered as the lock burst from the frame and the door was flung open.

Hannah glimpsed Jonathon Rowley with a fire poker in his hands, seconds before Wycliff launched himself forward and bowled the other man over.

A youth lay on the floor, blood seeping from a head wound. Were they too late?

Lady Gabriella squealed as her beau was knocked to the ground by the charging hellhound. Hannah stood in the doorway, not entirely sure what to do with herself. Her education as a quietly bred young lady had been deficient in fighting tactics. She might not be able to throw a punch, but there was one thing she could do—make sure the man's accomplice didn't escape.

"You!" Lady Gabriella spun and glared at her.

The two men exchanged blows that fell with the whack of fist against flesh. They picked themselves up off the floor, attacked, and crashed into a table that was pushed against the wall and under the sole window in the room.

"You will stay here, Lady Gabriella. You will stand trial for murder." Hannah pointed a finger and thought she sounded rather authoritative.

The lady in question laughed, a sneer on her face. "I am leaving and there is nothing you can do. I have the protection of my family."

Hannah wanted nothing more than to wipe the sneer from the young woman's face. Or even better, to reveal her for what she really was on the inside—rotten. Hannah reached out and snatched a length of ribbon. Not the wide silk one wound around the woman's hair, but the narrow one holding her delicate mask in place. Hannah tugged and the bow came undone.

"What are you doing?" Lady Gabriella raised her hands to her face and leaned away from Hannah until the ribbon tightened between them.

Hannah refused to yield the length of buttercream ribbon, the shade an exact match to her opponent's hair. Having untied it, she wound it around her finger and then yanked with all her might. The mask came free of the woman's face and as it fell, Hannah let go of the ribbon.

The porcelain shattered on the slate floor. Lady Gabriella gasped and swiped at Hannah but she jumped backwards, out of reach. The other woman's face had the characteristic blue-black patches of decomposition that gave her skin the appearance of mottled marble. She almost looked like a painting, if one had been left in the rain and the colours had run and merged together.

"You horrid creature! You'll pay for that. Just wait until my father hears of this." She picked up her skirts and elbowed Hannah to one side.

Hannah reached into the top of her stays and pulled the piece of paper free. Then she jumped at Lady Gabriella as though she played a childhood game of leap frog. She caught the other woman smack in the back and knocked her to the ground. Trying hard to forget about maintaining an air of calm dignity, Hannah sat on the other woman. With one hand, she lifted the hair free of the Afflicted woman's nape and pressed the paper to the exposed skin.

The words transferred themselves from paper to skin with a sibilant hiss. They glowed orange for a moment and then wriggled as though each letter were a tiny worm that burrowed into Lady Gabriella's body.

"What have you done?" She stopped struggling to throw Hannah off. The Afflicted woman's arms and legs fell still. Lady Gabriella didn't move as she muttered curses at Hannah. For a well-bred young lady, she had a particularly foul turn of phrase.

Hannah climbed off the prone woman and stood, keeping a tight grip on the slip of paper. She stepped over a knocked-over chair to check on the boy and ascertained he still breathed. Then she considered how to help Lord Wycliff.

The two men were still fighting their way around the room as though they were intent on destroying the lad's home. The table and chairs were knocked over. Blankets were pulled from the bed as they grappled with one another. It was a miracle they hadn't trampled the lad sprawled on the floor.

The viscount grabbed Rowley by the collar and shoved him up against a shelf that rattled the plates and cups it held. "I can do this all night, Wycliff, because my body repairs any damage you inflict and I do not tire. You cannot win." Rowley reached out with one hand, grabbed a plate from the shelf, and smashed it over the viscount's head.

Hannah studied Mr Rowley. With the benefit of hindsight, he displayed symptoms of addiction that could be mistaken for the beginnings of a fever or drunkenness. His eyes shone too brightly. His complexion was flushed and red. Sweat dribbled down his forehead. Although to be fair, there was some exertion involved in the fight. She marvelled that he displayed no rot, but then, he was eating to excess.

"Do you by chance have a plan, Miss Miles, since you have incapacitated Lady Gabriella?" the viscount asked as he blocked a punch and delivered one of his own.

"Yes. If you could hold Mr Rowley still?" She danced out of the way of the combatants. In the small space, it was difficult to stay out of their way and not stand on the unconscious boy. She cast a worried glance at the lad. He hadn't stirred, but other than reassuring herself that his chest rose and fell, Hannah couldn't afford just yet to tend to his head wound.

"I am trying," Lord Wycliff grunted as he wrestled the other man.

Rowley swung his arms, trying to dislodge the viscount. Wycliff grabbed him around the middle and refused to let go. He dug his shoulder into the other man's sternum and step by step, pushed him backwards to the wall.

"Gracious," Hannah whispered. The scientific part of her mind tried to calculate how much force the viscount had to exert to pin a frenzied Afflicted to the wall. He seemed very strong. Almost unnaturally so.

"I need him facing the wall so I can reach his neck," she said.

The viscount shot her a decidedly unamused glance. He took hold of Rowley's left hand and spun him, as though he led in a dance. The other man kicked out, but Wycliff took advantage of the momentary shift in balance. Keeping hold of Rowley's hand, Wycliff ducked under his arm and behind him. He pulled up the Afflicted man's arm as he spun and used it as leverage to drive them both into the wall.

Rowley cried out as his hand was dragged up his spine. With the viscount pressing on him, he was unable to wrest himself free.

"Now, Miss Miles! I cannot hold him for long."

Hannah stepped close, leaning against Lord Wycliff as she reached up and pressed the text to the back of Mr Rowley's neck. The words glowed as they sizzled against his skin. Then he grunted as each letter burrowed into him. He emitted a soft *oomph* as his knees gave way and he collapsed to the ground.

Wycliff stared at his fallen opponent, now prone at his feet. "What was that?"

"An immobilisation spell that my mother gave me." Hannah folded up the slip of paper, careful to keep all the text on the inside, before she slipped it back into the top of her stays.

The viscount tugged on the points of his waistcoat as he adjusted his clothing. "How long will it last?"

"Two hours for mice. I cannot say how long for them." Hannah stared at the viscount. Blood dribbled down his temple and his lip was split on one side. His black hair was terribly dishevelled and a button was missing from his waistcoat. He looked terrible...and yet rather more human at the same time.

"I'll fetch some rope from the stables and alert the staff." He ducked through the open door and was swallowed by the dark.

Hannah knelt next to the lad and pressed two fingers against his neck. She was reassured to find a strong pulse. A quick examination revealed no other wounds apart from the gash to his temple and a large lump where his head must have hit the ground. Hannah folded her handkerchief into a neat square and pressed it to the cut. "You will live, young man, assuming there is no permanent damage from the blow. Though it might require stitches, from the look of it."

Wycliff returned with a length of rope and dragged first Mr Rowley and then Lady Gabriella to the middle of the room. "I found a servant coming to investigate the shouting. I sent him to fetch the authorities."

"Do you need medical attention?" Hannah took stock of the viscount's injuries.

Wycliff had taken several blows and been hit over the head with an assortment of belongings. Blood and scratches marred the hard planes of his face. He waved her hand away. "I've suffered worse and lived."

They soon had both Afflicted secured, hands tied behind their backs and arms bound to their torsos. They propped the two against each other, still unable to wriggle so much as a fingertip, but somewhat revived. Lady Gabriella cursed them both.

"I love you, Gabriella," Mr Rowley declared, unable to see the woman lashed to his back.

Cold eyes glared at Hannah. "Oh, do be quiet, Rowley. My father will have us released as soon as he hears."

"No. He won't." Wycliff crossed his arms and examined his broken fingernails. "You will both be charged with murder, but given your Afflicted status, you will be dealt with by the Ministry of Unnaturals. Your father cannot help you now."

Mr Rowley turned into a blubbering mess now that he was captured. "You cannot blame me. Gabriella did this to me. You must feed me. The hunger is agony and it tears me apart. I require sustenance. The boy is a mere servant—he is no loss to the world." His eyes rolled up in their sockets until only the white showed, and an angry edge crept into his words.

"I told you to be quiet," Lady Gabriella hissed.

"I might be able to assist you, Mr Rowley. Might I enquire how long have you been one of the Afflicted?" Hannah asked. The opportunity to question an Afflicted in the grips of a mad hunger but not yet unintelligible was too great to allow to pass.

His lips pulled back and he bit out each word as though he suffered a great deal of pain. "A little over a month."

"Did you attempt a normal feeding regime of a sliver a day?" How she wished she had her notebook to record his responses.

He sneered. "I starve and you expect me to be satisfied with a mere wafer? I am a man with large appetites."

In three weeks he had consumed as many minds. With no self-control, his hunger would continue to escalate even as his outward condition deteriorated. They should be grateful only three people had died and no more.

"Lady Gabriella, if you had any regard for your companion, how could you do this?" Hannah tried to puzzle out the other woman. How could a woman kill the man she professed to love? It made no sense.

Lady Gabriella snorted. "You will never understand, with your little mind and your boring, pointless existence. Rowley shares my appetites for many things. Together, we experience ecstasy beyond your comprehension. Servants are the cattle we feed upon in order to live forever and an aftermage tastes so much sweeter."

Hannah rankled at the insult. She most certainly did *not* have a little mind. With regard to the topic of the Afflicted, she knew far more than Lady Gabriella. "You won't live forever, and you have killed Mr Rowley twice. Once when you infected him with your old face powder, and he will die a second time within the next few months."

"You don't know what you are talking about." An eye roll dismissed Hannah as effectively as if the noblewoman had turned her back.

"On the contrary, I do. My father and I have discovered that the curse in the powder deteriorates over time. A woman infected six months ago recently dropped completely dead. Her heart had rotted inside her body. If he follows the same pattern, Mr Rowley will succumb to internal rot before the year is out."

"What?" Mr Rowley exclaimed. His eyes widened as he tried to glare at the woman behind him.

At that moment soldiers appeared in the doorway. "Viscount Wycliff?" the sergeant asked.

Wycliff drew papers from his jacket pocket. "I am authorised by the Ministry of Unnaturals to investigate two recent murders. These two are responsible. I require that you take them into custody at the garrison. They must be kept most securely as they are Afflicted and dangerous. No one is to be allowed near them until I arrange for them to be moved to a location controlled by the Ministry of Unnaturals."

As the soldiers took hold of the bound couple, Hannah knelt by the boy, who stirred. "I will take the lad to my father. His wound needs tending."

Wycliff carried the limp boy to the Loburn carriage and laid him on the seat. Then Hannah climbed up into the carriage and sat next to him.

Wycliff grasped the handle of the door. "I wanted to say thank you, Miss Miles, for your assistance in this matter. I do not believe the two responsible would have been captured without you."

Before Hannah could muster up an answer, he had closed the door and tapped the side to signal the driver to move off.

Hannah stared at the unconscious boy. "Who would have thought that the wraith could ever say thank you?"

A warm glow spread through her torso. Even stranger than his words was the effect they had on her. She kept a close eye on the boy as the carriage pulled her toward home. He murmured in his enforced sleep and Hannah reached out to stroke his brow, hoping it might soothe him somewhat.

With a gasp, the boy seized her hand and his eyes flew open. He stared at their joined hands and then up at her face.

"I'm so sorry, miss," he whispered, his brown eyes wide.

Hannah swallowed the lump in her throat as she recalled the boy's magical gift. He could tell with a single touch what ailed a person. She managed to form her lips into a smile. "Don't you worry about me. We must tend to your head."

Without another word, he slipped back into the embrace of unconsciousness.

# 23

The carriage had barely rolled to a stop when Sir Hugh wrenched open the door.

"Are you all right, Hannah?" He peered into the dim interior.

Hannah gestured to her charge. "I am perfectly well, but this lad has a cut to his head from a poker and an egg-shaped lump from hitting the floor. He has been drifting in and out of consciousness."

"Let's get him inside." Her father reached in and gathered the slim boy in his large arms. "Sera alerted me that you had used her spell. Twice."

Hannah followed her father up the path. "Two Afflicted were behind the murders. One is a man, a Mr Jonathon Rowley, who was infected a month ago by Lady Gabriella Ridlington. We must secure and destroy the face powder she used."

"Poor bugger. If the curse manifests in him the

way it did in the maid, he will drop by midsummer. What symptoms does he manifest?"

Mary stood on the front porch holding aloft a lantern. She stepped aside as they passed within.

"He is in the grips of addiction and it seems he arose with a strong hunger that could not be sated by the regular amount. One brain a week, shared with Lady Gabriella, has been insufficient to ease his craving. To look at him, he appears to have a fever, with bright eyes and a flush to his skin." Hannah followed her father across the hall.

"I wonder at what point the fevered look succumbs to rot?" Sir Hugh said.

Hannah could imagine her father already anticipating the study of Mr Rowley and his slide into decline and permanent death.

Another revelation from the evening niggled at Hannah. "Mr Rowley said he had large appetites for all things and Lady Gabriella said that she infected him in order to share her appetites and its...ecstasy. This seems to confirm that those who are dangerous have a predisposition for indulging to excess." Hannah wondered what pleasure they found in the process of killing an innocent person and devouring their warm, fresh brain. To find bliss in such a monstrous act was indeed unnatural and in this instance, she shared Viscount Wycliff's disgust for the Afflicted.

Her father grunted. "Unfortunately, Hannah,

there is a type of pleasure found in gluttony for some Afflicted. I'm sure your mother can explain it to you."

A small front room often served as a surgery for those who sought Sir Hugh out at home. Hannah opened the door while Mary activated the mushroom lamps. Sir Hugh laid the boy on the day bed and he muttered as his mind struggled to resurface.

Hannah sent Mary to fetch warm water and cloths to clean the wound while her father examined the cut. Then she retrieved the rolled pouch that contained his needles and thread.

Her father bent over his patient. "The lad is lucky he had a tough head. He will have a rakish scar to entice the ladies when he is older."

A half dozen stitches sealed the cut, then a bandage was wound around the youth's head.

"The boy has a most interesting gift. He can tell what ails a person by touching them," Hannah said as she pulled a blanket over him.

Her father looked up, excitement lighting his face. "Really? Do you think he would be interested in pursuing a career in medicine?"

Hannah bit back a smile. Sir Hugh had long sought an apprentice who was an aftermage. "He is currently a stable boy, but he may be open to a change of profession. Particularly if it means fewer people trying to bash in his skull with a poker."

The boy awoke with a startled gasp and sat up.

One hand went to the bandage wrapped around his head.

"You have stitches, but will heal," Hannah said gently. "This is my father, Sir Hugh Miles. He is a doctor and would like to examine you, now that you are awake."

The lad's wide eyes drifted sideways to her father, then he nodded.

"What's your name, lad?" Sir Hugh asked.

"Timothy, sir." The boy's voice was faint.

Sir Hugh peered into the lad's wide eyes. "Do you have family we should contact, to let them know you are well?"

The lad shook his head while trying to keep his attention on the doctor. "No, sir. I'm an orphan. Lord Byrd took me in as a stable boy."

Sir Hugh stood up and crossed his large arms. "Waste of your magic gift, if you don't mind my saying so. Have you ever considered a career in medicine?"

The boy laughed and snatched at the blanket covering his body. A tremor ran through his thin form from the shock of his encounter. "How would a gutter rat like me ever get the book learning to do that?"

Sir Hugh grinned. "I have a proposition for you, Timothy. If you were my apprentice, I would pay for your education and train you as a doctor. In return, all I would ask is that you use your gift to help both my research and the unfortunates who seek me out. You would also, naturally, be a member of our household."

The next day, a note was sent to Lord Byrd to advise him that his stable boy was under Sir Hugh's care and would not be returning to his position in that household. Instead, Timothy settled into his new life at Westbourne Green.

IN THE WEEK THAT FOLLOWED, an expedited trial was held for Mr Rowley and Lady Gabriella Ridlington. Even her father's influence failed to rescue her when it was revealed that she consumed the brains of servants for the pleasure of it. Necessity was understandable. Lust was not.

Both were sentenced to be interred at the Repository of Forgotten Things. For Mr Rowley, it would be a short sentence, and Sir Hugh waited for the day he would be laid out on the autopsy table. Lady Gabriella would become a nightmare creature, pacing her small cell until such time as they either discovered a cure, or she finally surrendered to death.

Seraphina was as excited to have a new thread to research as Hannah's father was to employ his apprentice. Hannah had raised the possible relevance of the heart as the seat of the soul and the reason the Afflicted remained conscious and ambulatory without circulation. Seraphina was delighted to delve into Egyptian history and religion.

While her mother studied the magical practices of Egyptian mages, Hannah read of the practical methods they employed to tend their dead. Squinting over tiny text kept her mind from Lord Wycliff and what had happened to him during the war. Or the warmth that had bloomed through her chest when he thanked her for her assistance.

A week later, Hannah sat in the front parlour with an open book, but her mind wandered to thoughts of dogs. Or rather, puppies. She had turned a page without looking as she found her mind drifting to places that had no bearing on their research, when there was a loud and determined rap on the front door.

She placed a marker in her book and set it on the sofa. "Whoever can that be?"

She opened the door herself, since Mary was busy elsewhere. On the porch was a most startling sight.

Viscount Wycliff stood on the doorstep, along with a modest amount of luggage. Hannah reverted to the state she had suffered from on their first meeting, and could find no words to string together. She just stared at him.

"I am accepting your mother's invitation," he said, bringing their staring contest to an end.

"My mother's invitation?" Hannah turned as her

father wheeled Seraphina's bath chair out into the hall.

Seraphina gestured for the viscount to come in. "Excellent! You have chosen to accept. Hannah can show you to your rooms."

Lord Wycliff picked up his bags and stepped around the frozen Hannah.

"Rooms?" What was going on here? Recent events had turned their quiet and orderly lives upside down, but surely not this much.

"Yes, his rooms, dearest. I suggested that it would be most convenient if Lord Wycliff were to reside here to help our research into the Afflicted. There is much to be done, and this saves both parties' travelling back and forth from London. There is a suite on the second floor he can occupy, and an empty room on the first he can use as his personal study."

"Viscount Wycliff is going to live here?" Surely her mother jested.

Seraphina's veil drifted back and forth as she laughed. "You always did complain this house was too big, Hannah. As a child, you asked constantly for playmates to fill these rooms."

She had yearned for friends to play hide and seek with in the backyard forest. Not a dark wraith who would spread gloom wherever he went.

"Sir Manly was most appreciative of your help in capturing Lady Gabriella and Mr Rowley, Miss Miles," the wraith said. "He thought you might be of assistance in my other ongoing investigations. That is, if you do not mind widening your studies of Unnatural creatures." For once the man didn't frown or glare, but had an open expression on his face, as though these were his first tentative steps toward being civilised.

Hannah shut the door and stared at the viscount. She had wanted a puppy, but her mother had presented her with a hellhound.

It remained to be seen if he would be the bearer of death or a devoted guardian. As Hannah's shock faded, she found herself relishing the prospect of finding out.

## THE END

Hannah will be back with a new murder to solve in book 2...

# GALVANISM AND GHOULS

*Time reveals all secrets*

A new unnatural horror is about to rattle Hannah Miles' quiet existence, and it's not the short-tempered viscount prowling the hallways. Someone is creating a monster by stitching together pieces of different people. When a limb makes an escape attempt, Viscount Wycliff is called to investigate. All of London knows there is one mad scientist among them capable of creating such an ungodly monster... Sir Warren Miles.

Hannah's father is suspected of a most heinous crime and she is determined to clear his name, even as Wycliff works to see the murderer hang. Buried secrets that touch all their lives will be brought to the surface. One such secret belongs to Hannah and could tear her world apart.

With Hannah and Wycliff on opposing sides, can they find the real monster and will it be the hand that wields the scalpel, or the creature hiding in the dark?

# Did you enjoy MANNERS and MONSTERS?

Thanks so much for reading *Manners and Monsters* and I hope you enjoyed it.

Please consider taking a moment to share your thoughts by leaving a review at the retailer where you purchased this book. Reader reviews help other readers discover new books.

*Thank you,* Tilly

# ABOUT THE AUTHOR

Tilly drinks entirely too much coffee, likes to watch Buffy the Vampire Slayer and wishes she could talk to Jane Austen. Sometimes she imagines a world where the Bennet sisters lived near the Hellmouth. Or that might be a fanciful imagining brought on by too much caffeine.

To be the first to hear about new releases and special offers sign up at:
www.tillywallace.com/newsletter

*Tilly would love to hear from you:*
www.tillywallace.com
tilly@tillywallace.com

facebook.com/tillywallaceauthor

bookbub.com/authors/tilly-wallace